# Creative Writing Heals
# Volume 6

A new collection from Converge writers
at York St John University 2023

Creative Writing Heals: Volume 6
First published in 2023
by Writing Tree Press



For information contact:
Writing Tree Press, Unit 10773, PO Box 4336
Manchester, M61 0BW
www.writingtree.co.uk

# Contents

# Foreword

This has been a very exciting year for us in Converge Creative Writing. For the first time we offered a Creative Writing conference for our colleagues and fellow students at York St John University and the wider academic community. We enjoyed keynote speeches from Professor Abi Curtis and Dr Liesl King from York St John, a series of readings from Creative Writing Heals writers and excellent workshops by our Converge Creative Writing students. It was a true celebration of writing and a showcase of talent. I'd like to say a big thank you to our writers who contributed and made it such a great day.

At the conference I shared some numbers about Creative Writing Heals contributors. I am delighted to add Creative Writing Heals 6 to our roster of anthologies. It brings our total number of pieces published to 270, and our authors to 100! In this year's volume you will find a veritable smorgasbord of writing: poetry, fiction, life writing and essays, in genres from crime fiction to dark fairy fantasy.

It's a huge pleasure, as always, to see our writers grow in skill and confidence. I hope you enjoy the feast they have created for you here!

Helen Kenwright
*Converge Creative Writing Lead & Writing Tree Director*

*December 2023*

*"Finding a voice means that you can get your own feeling into your own words and that your words have the feel of you about them."*
*– Seamus Heaney*

# It's a small world (but I wouldn't like to paint it).

## Kevin Keld

I find it all rather creepy and just a little bit weird when faced with coincidences on an unprecedented level. I genuinely believe that it could be some kind of malevolent and unseen or alien force directing the atoms of one person/place/thing to collide unceremoniously with similar atoms of an identical person/place/thing. Could it be written in our stars? Could it be written in your stars? (As read by some portly gentleman in an ill-fitting but colourful cardigan in the delightfully deranged Daily Express). However you choose to explain it, I appear to have suffered, or perhaps enjoyed, more than my fair share of coincidences over the past sixty years, and it does not include the little gem that both myself and my first wife were brought into this world on the same day.

So here for your perusal and inspection are some of my atom colliding events. For the sake of brevity, I will list only the top three: Cue Top of the Pops theme music from the 1970s.

*This week's number three - up five places from last week's eight - it's Yours Truly with The Plane in Spain.*

Whilst travelling back to the UK from Valencia some eighteen years ago, I was embarrassingly heralded by a loud and unruly middle-aged guy sitting at the rear of the almost full Boeing 727.

'Eyup Keldy, what are you doing on here?'

I resisted the urge to reply with such flippant remarks as 'I'm scaling the heights of Mount Etna in a diamond studded tutu,' or 'I'm building a scale model of the Starship Enterprise from strawberry jam.' I chose instead to just shrug my shoulders and look as innocent as I could. However, I was pleasantly surprised to see that the voice belonged to one of my long-time customers, Les. (Name *not* changed for the sake of anonymity.)

After battling his way past the overloaded in-flight Dick Turpin trolley, he launched himself into the vacant seat on my left, just in time to order a large Scotch from the passing Judas. Les explained that he was now flying back to East Yorkshire with a copy of the deeds to his fresh, new residence, having just sold his soul to pay the deposit on an idyllic country property with its own swimming pool and obligatory palm trees. After a thirty-minute detailed description of the new bungalow and its surrounding area, Les managed to take a breather and sink the previously ignored Scotch and water in one hit. I instantly grasped my chance to involve myself in the conversation.

'Well believe it or not, the ink is still wet on the contract for the house that we have just bought too, complete with a private swimming pool and *five* palm trees,' I added childishly. 'Oh really, and where have you decided to "lay your hat"?' spluttered Les, reaching for the drained Scotch glass. He was frustrated because the drinks trolley had now finished its tour of duty having made enough money to purchase a small island off the coast of Mexico.

'A tiny agricultural village that you probably haven't heard of called Montroi, half an hour's drive from the city.'

From the look on his face you could easily believe that I had told him that his cat had "inappropriately" rubbed itself against the vacuum cleaner, wearing a "kiss me quick" hat.

'Why the face of despair Les?' I cheerily asked.

'Montroi' he spluttered. 'Montroi, I know it, it's where I shall be living for the next few years.... it's where I have bought our house!'

So, for many years I lived in the same village in Spain as one of my customers. The stories from that section of my life would make interesting reading, but we must move on.

*And in this week's second place - down from the top slot last week - is The Trouble with Uncle Malcolm.*

As a child in the 1960s, I was very much captivated by my father's brother, Malcolm. He was the traditional 'rough diamond' of the family, and someone whose dubious drunken antics I really aspired to. I have spent years trying to live up to his reputation as the ultimate black sheep of the family whilst being thought of as nothing worse than a scamp. Unfortunately, the passage of time and various family tragedies meant that for the best part of forty years, our paths never crossed and Malcolm and I lost touch. The very fact that I had moved to live in another country didn't help matters. Moving up to the Summer of 2022, and you would find me sitting in a café in my home town of Driffield. Peering above my shameful cup of Americano I spied a chap who looked remarkably like my uncle. I was far too nervous to blatantly ask him, 'Hey, are you my uncle?' but as I was departing the café, perhaps missing the chance of a reunion forever, my partner, Vanessa, pressurized me into introducing myself to the elderly gent. She stressed that, judging by his age, he might not be drinking industrial strength coffee in here for much longer and in the words of Mrs Doyle she advised me to go on, go on, go on, (Father Ted aficionados will know). I approached him with the feeling that I was being sent to the headmaster for punishment, but after carefully studying his features I gingerly asked, 'Excuse me but is your name Malcolm?'

I hadn't expected his immediate reply of 'Yes, Kevin, it is.' It was indeed my long-lost uncle, and after inviting myself to his table for the best part of an hour, the subject turned to where he called home these days.

'In Driffield now,' he proudly announced after listing living in just about every town in the Northern

Hemisphere.

'Wow, so do I. I live with my daughter in a peaceful part of town called Curlew Close'.

At this, his jaw hit the floor and once again had that look on his face reminiscent of someone who has been smacked across the chops with a four-stone sack of wet kippers. 'Why that's exactly where I live,' he eventually murmured. 'At number three.'

Well, for the record I can tell you that I live at number five and have done for three years.

By far the scariest, spine-tingling, bottom-twitching coincidence is yet to surface. In a tiny bar/restaurant in downtown Orlando, over in The Sunshine State of Florida; I was living at the time with a partner on an isolated farm up in the dreamy, picturesque Yorkshire Wolds. My partner was nominated by a co-worker to receive an all-expenses jaunt for the whole family to Universal Studios in Florida, for her sterling work in the community and all courtesy of Ant and Dec's popular TV show, *Saturday Night Takeaway*. The only stipulation was that we would have to take part in the show. Sounds easy, doesn't it? It would have been fabulous, had they not proceeded to film the live show in the 38-degree sunshine. It was an afternoon spent trying to avoid becoming a salty, muddy puddle seeping through the stage. After consuming the whole of the water ration for the state of Florida, I was then constantly in need of the restroom, and so it went on, fill up with water, thirty seconds of filming, then a race for the sanctuary of the nearest portaloo. As the day came to a welcome close it was decided that we would head off with some American friends into the darkest depths of downtown Orlando in search of a hearty meal, namely a steak the size of a Dutch paratrooper's left boot with numerous gallons of cool, tasty beer to follow, topped off with a dessert that would scream five-pound weight gain just by looking at it.

We left the main street and eventually pulled into a lively place called the Steakhouse Blues, complete with its flashing neon sign depicting a rather small but soulful bull crooning into a fifties-style microphone. I can only presume he was wailing out some ancient, tearful blues number and not "Agadoo". What on earth were we letting ourselves in for? The row of enormous dust-covered four-by-fours outside lent a certain threatening atmosphere to the place. Could it perhaps be bustling with the local cowboy community whose sole Saturday evening entertainment was to disembowel tourists who had wandered off the beaten track? There was only one way to find out, so in a rare act of chivalry I held the door open for everyone else to enter whilst bringing up the rear - just in case we encountered any vicious-looking cowboys searching for their next hide. I had no need for concern: the place was full of dimly lit, secluded booths packed with hungry families tucking into burgers the size of a dustbin lid. The clacking of pool balls emanated from below the neon sign that originally advised Budweiser-drinking customers to 'get it here', but with the letters G and E missing from the beginning. It was the only area in the place that wasn't reserved for hungry customers stabbing their food with steely knives. We were swiftly shown to an ample-sized table by a pretty waitress who was about as interested in serving us as she would be to have a leg amputated.

Through a chewing gum laden mouth, she uttered the very welcoming words, 'Drinks?' Of course, it would be rude not to partake after such a scorchingly hot afternoon's filming, so an eight-pint jug of best American beer was ordered and at once we were delving into the menu to see what bovine delights we could attack, allowing a minuscule partition on the plate for a salad, of course. It was then that I spied a rather unusual drinking device on the adjacent table. A group of six eaters were studying a tall glass - and when I say tall it was four feet tall with the circumference of a pint glass - and at the bottom of the glass was a miniature tap. The whole thing was filled halfway with a refreshing light brown liquid, quite obviously beer. Being the inquisitive soul that I am, I inquired of the forty-something lady closest to me what the purpose of the tall glass might be. She had no idea, other than it being some kind of gimmick laid on by the management to sell even more units of their dreadful beer. I found that after the initial drink had quenched the thirst very satisfactorily then the second took on the taste and texture of the stale liquid found in the garden bird bath. It was immediately apparent that these people spoke with an English accent not unlike my own, and after a few rounds of 'chewing the fat', as they say in the good 'ol US of A, the conversation came around to the obligatory, 'Whereabouts in the UK are you guys from?'

The lady next to me, who had taken on the role of speaker for the whole table, informed me that they were on a two-week holiday and home for them was in Yorkshire.

'Same here,' says yours truly, quite surprised that we both lived in the same county. 'In fact, it's not far from Hull, a little village called Everingham, we always say Hull because it's the nearest big city.'

Hmmm, I thought, this is going to become worthy of an episode of The Twilight Zone with an ageing Rod Serle burbling his narrative at the beginning.

'Well, believe it or not, I know Everingham. I live in Pocklington, a little under five miles away,' I excitedly announced. 'I used to own a motorcycle business on Pocklington Industrial Estate,' I added and at this point, the lady looked as shocked as I must have appeared to her and with a croaky, nervous voice said, 'Kevin, you are Kevin Keld, you are acquainted with my father Neville, the local haulier!'

'I am indeed, and yes, I do know your father.'

I'd love to be able to say we all fell around laughing rather like they do at the end of a Scooby Doo episode when the fiendish villain has been unmasked, but alas everyone was so damned hungry and thirsty that we continued to order more of the disgusting beer - I think it was called Garden Mulch- and ate medium rare steaks the size of a cowboy hat.

I'll never forget the chance meeting in that bar so many miles from home, and as Bogart wearily announced, 'Of all the gin joints in all the towns in all the world she had to walk into mine.'

# COVID Fox

## John F. Goodfellow

Postman Geoff
Told me a fox
Used to walk up Coney Street
Bold as brass, day and night

At night on the Estate foxes and students compete
To gain my attention
For all the world, alien babies being born.

Ginsberg's Howl has nothing on them!
Singing stale lullabies to each other
As I had in Coventry all those years ago
When plague and pox were something others had.

So the Fox walks among us now and we put out cat food for her.
She digs up my blood and bone and scutters my new hedge.

Shit! She's here again.
Get Out!

But look, she wants to be friends.
Do I have enough friends?

# Glass Teeth

## Michael Fairclough

A door slammed, disturbing me. Stretching out from the bed to pull my curtains to, I knocked over a glass of water trying to save myself some sleep. Waking up around noon, I was hungover and needed a wee. Sitting on my toilet, I went over the events of last night as I had no idea how I had gotten home.

'Not a taxi,' I muttered, as I could feel my emergency note in my sock.

'And I always miss the last bus.' I headed back into my room and remembered the glass I had knocked over. Unusual for me, I picked it up, the water having dried and that's when I saw them. The teeth, fake but yellowed and set in replica gums. One web search later, I had a list of places where I might discover the identity of my reverse tooth fairy. That or some promiscuous pensioners at least. I just hoped I hadn't been robbing graves drunk again.

Starting with the obvious, I popped over to the dentist.

'Name?'

'Stephanie.'

'We don't have any appointments for Stephanie.'

'I don't have one. I just need to ask some questions about these teeth,' I said holding them to her face. Only for her to whack my arm away.

'If you don't have an appointment, you can't see the dentist, now please leave.' Angry, I brayed on the receptionist's desk demanding to see the tooth touchier. She was appointment-only though and all booked up. Frustrated, I snapped a giant toothbrush they had on display. Then stormed out shouting, 'Get cavities, you appointment-keeping knob!'

Outside, I tried to calm down. In hindsight though they probably had some sort of dentist/patient confidentiality. Not sure why, it's not like you can say much with your mouth full of fingers. Also, if you're confiding in your dentist, you should seek professional help. Like a mistress or an assassin.

After that I sneaked past the library to the charity shop and their resident wrinkled woman. (Having borrowed *Fifty Shades* on the misconception it was about elephant poaching, I was too embarrassed to return it.) Picking up a donated urn I grabbed some ashes from inside before blowing them into their face and used the ensuing sneeze to look inside their mouth. Alas, they still had their teeth but, determined to make the most of it, I bought the urn to hold my new toilet brush.

Next, I tried the bingo hall. Unfortunately, my ex-partner Brenda worked there as a caller and we'd ended on bad terms. She was okay for the most part. But if she was not shouting 'Two fat ladies!' when we were getting intimate, or 'Bingo!' when she finished, she would complain about the amount of people at the get-togethers after. Now don't get me wrong, they were packed and it did take place in a bungalow, but it was hardly a full house. At most the living room and the bedroom were full. Always a line for the bog though. Not realising these habits annoyed me, she made the effort to change, but got mad when she started calling out our alternative phrases at work. Such as.

'Two sentient beings who are trying hard to get into shape and all this vigorous, yet still passionate intercourse is helping. 88... pounds is what we spent collectively at Weight Watchers before quitting to continue our new sexercise plan.' Which I can't blame her for, as they nearly fired her over it, it being 'bring your grandchildren to bingo' afternoon. Ultimately, it was my fault we broke up, as through bingo I discovered my interest in older women.

Waiting at the back of the hall, I listened out for any sloppy announcements of 'full house!' or 'bingo'. But to my dismay there was not a recognisable word to be heard, it being Super Shot Saturday, meaning they were all hammered and in no mood for me to inspect their gummy maws. Also, the first four I approached tried to bite me. Not one to give up, I withdrew and waited for Brenda to finish her shift.

Noticing me, she made eye contact from the stage. All the while remaining the consummate professional.

'Eighty-five, the age you will die. Seventy-two, It's a home for you. Thirty-three, what do you want Stephanie?'

'Full house!' An old woman shouted, before struggling to stand up to swear at her competition. Her card being a winner, they took a break to check it and Brenda came over.

'Stephanie.'

'Brenda.'

'Still alive I see.'

'Yes... Still shouting at elderly people, I see.'

'What do you want?'

'Listen, I hate to do this but have any of your players lost their dentures recently?'

'What the hell are you on about?'

'Look, just answer the question.'

'Ugh, if a player shows up without their teeth, we refuse entry on grounds that they've had enough and have probably lost them. If they misplace them while here, they go in lost property and are used as prizes when we do the Christmas raffle.'

'I see,' I said, then promptly left as I had no further questions and it was getting awkward.

Next, I popped by Betty's. The line being what it was, I decided it was not worth the wait. If I ran out of options, I would just accost someone when they left later.

By the time I got to the post office I was desperate. Waiting in the queue I took the opportunity to trip every old dear as they passed. Blaming the carpet as I helped them up, I used the opening to check their mugs out for teeth. Squeezing their faces between my hands, I put on an air of concern all the while telling them, 'You should be careful at your age, now off you pop. Coro is on later.' Only for them to reply with some version of, 'Okay love, but please stop, you are crushing my frail skull,' through a squished-up mouth, revealing if they had their teeth or not. Several tripped nans later, only two did not have their teeth. One saying, 'she blends her food' and the other saying; 'I'm getting gold caps fitted and between you and me I hate my children. Not a redeeming thing about them and if they think they are getting owt, they have another thing coming. Selfish little shits. Actually, what do you think would be the biggest waste of money?' She said while pulling photos out of her purse of mock-up mausoleums and coffins, each more garish than the last. Decorated in gold, and diamonds. She had no intention of actually buying them. But the photos were what she liked to call: 'Psychological warfare. Then next chance I get I'm fleeing to Mexico. The way I see it, I already have the texture of wrinkled old leather so I may as well get a tan to complete the look. Also, it's a lovely country with rich cultural heritage and beautiful scenery. You know like Americans thought England was like before the rise of the Internet?' It was during this I become first in line, but was unable to break free of her mesmerizing rambling, as every time I tried to turn away, she would drag me back in, getting ever more familiar. Thankfully, the spell was soon broken as another elderly woman walked by the post office and a rather potent smell came in on the breeze.

'Etty, you cheating old flapper! She told me she was being put into a home. So, she couldn't come to my Rodger's funeral.' At that she stormed out after her. Determination in her wonky stride after her hip surgery last summer. That settled I approached the counter.

'Look I have wasted enough time today show me your teeth.'

'No,' The woman behind the counter said. Shaking her head.

'I'm warning you don't make me force you to, I'm not in the mood.'

'Nope, not going to happen.' Angry at her dismissiveness, I pounced like a tiger only for the dividing pane to act as a shield for the old woman, deflecting my attack. Regaining my composure, I took some deep breaths and tried again.

'Show me your teeth. I would like to see them.'

'No.'

'For goodness' sake, why the hell not? It's not like I'm trying to rob you. I just want to see in your moist mouth.'

'You didn't say please.'

'Oh, was that it?'

'Yep, common human decency.'

'Oh well, I can manage that. Please show me inside your mouth.'

Another one checked off my list and another dead end. I was starting to think all was lost. But that's when it came to me, pure inspiration.

At the hospital, I headed straight for the dementia ward. It struck me that dentures sounded a lot like dementia in a funny voice. Also, it's common in the elderly. (Not funny voices, then again Orville is getting on for a duck.) To think at any other time, I would be angry at the current state of the NHS. But when you're trespassing with nefarious intent it's useful for nurses and doctors to be understaffed and overworked. On the ward, I tried not draw attention to myself and quietly made my way into the first room. Inside the lights were dim and an old woman sat up in bed watching the TV.

'Hey, Grandma.'

'Natalie, is that you?'

'Yea it's me, come to visit you.'

'Yes, that's right. You said you would. Won't be long now before I can go home, I should think.'

'Yea I imagine so,' I said, getting close enough now to pull up a chair at the side of her bed. 'Wow, Grandma, what great big ears you have,' I said, lost in her droopy lobes.

'What did you say?' she said, in a tone that I was unsure if was anger or confusion.

'I said what great big eyes you have, Grandma.'

'Well yes, the doctor said they're dilated. It's a reaction to my medication. That paired with convex lenses I look higher than your father when he got back after that concert.'

'Oh really?' I replied before moving on to the final question in my devious plan.

'Yes, not that I mind in hindsight. Come to think of it, I should be due some drugs myself soon.'

'Speaking of things you can stick in your mouth, may I have a look in yours, Grandma?' Looking at me puzzled, she simply shrugged before opening wide to reveal no teeth to be found.

'Wow Grandma, what big teeth you don't have. I don't suppose you would like to try these?' I said, pulling out the yellowed gnashers.

'What on earth are you doing with them? And of course, I would not have teeth in. Who the hell are you?' Rumbled, I tried one last time to get her on side.

'It's me Grandma Natalie, you know Natalie blah blahs

daughter.'

'Shut up, I'm no fool. Anyone who knows me knows I hate dentists. Bunch of perverts the lot of them, with their knock-out gas and rubber gloves. Get out of my sight and take your fake teeth with you, before I buzz a nurse.'

Taking the teeth, I left the old woman in the knowledge that I hadn't seen a single member of staff between the elevator and the ward. That and her buzzer was the button from a cheap doorbell. In the hallway I lost all motivation to try another room. So left to head home defeated by the mystery and depressed by the state of health care in our country.

Outside the hospital, I leant on a nearby bus stop, exhausted from my day of investigation. But looking down the road for the bus coming, I found all was not lost as, just like a nativity, three weirdly dressed old folk came up to me. Lollipop-people, a job made up almost exclusively of the elderly.

'Stop!' I shouted, as I used my body to block the path in front of them, using their anti-car tactics against them.

'You shall not pass, unless you show me your teeth… please.' Confused but agreeable, the first opened his mouth to show me.

Then he said, 'They're fake, but most of me is. See my eye? It's glass, lost it to a man wielding a spoon. Got a false hip as well, lost my left arm to a bus and I sat on my right leg funny one day and they had to amputate. Even my hair colour is a lie.' He pulled off a wig to show me where he had dyed it black.

'Oh, and I nearly forgot this.' He pulled his high-vis open to show me his left nipple.

'Touch it, go on, it won't lactate, I promise.' Reaching for the lollipop-man's nipple, my finger went further than expected and as his nipple flattened, the illusion was broken.

'Lost it to breast cancer. Did you know one in a hundred UK males get breast cancer every year? So anyhow, I got this tattoo after they amputated my left nip. Great, isn't it?'

Only for one of the lollipop-women to interrupt, 'No, he's lying! He lies about everything - well apart from the cancer. We had a fundraiser and Janet ran a marathon. But the rest is lies, and the teeth are mine, now give them to me!' she screeched, through a perfect set of teeth. Ignoring her, I turned to the last a scrawny specimen.

'What about you? Are they your teeth and if so, can you prove it?' Ringing her hands together, the runt of the litter began her piece.

'Why yes, they're my teeth and if you turn them over, you'll see my mother wrote my name on the gums.'

'And how do I know that's your name? Do you have any Identification?' I responded. Only for her to reach into her jacket and pull out a bra with a matching name on it. That settled, all that was left was to shove her teeth back in. So, restraining her head between my thick thighs, I took the opportunity to look into her extremely green eyes. But I couldn't help but feel that we were not meant to be. Then again, I had never done it with a lollipop-person before. A rare opportunity to be sure, having not interacted with one since I was in school, and then as my protector when I crossed the road. That morning though, she had gone without even a whisper. Fleeing off into the council estate on a mobility scooter, or maybe she got the bus? She would have to pay before 9am though. That would not explain how I got back home though. So maybe she did use a mobility scooter and I could have sat on her lap.

I kind of want to sit on Mrs Santa's lap now. I hope she knows I've been naughty this year...

*Glass Teeth* Illustration by Michael Fairclough

# meeting

## james mcnally

how old is this place
maybe sixties
but the fear the apprehension
is the same I think
as through the ages

we enter with our own thoughts
congesting in our own minds
we sit in awkward poses

the room is bland
of necessity maybe
for the words are not
they are frighteningly and
appallingly real

time and space
and circumstance
become awful

the meeting at fulford police station
16 november 2022

# The Last Case of Detective Bane

## Junior Mark Cryle

Lightning flashed and thunder roared throughout the mansion. Its gothic aesthetics appeared more gruesome and terrifying as a result, which did not calm the nerves of the current occupants.

They numbered six in total: two smartly-dressed men and two elegant-looking women sat together at the dining table, another man in a tux holding a tray of refreshments, and the last man pacing back and forth in contemplation, undisturbed by the weather that frightened the rest.

'You're probably wondering why I, Detective Bane, have called you all here to the scene of the crime.' He ceased his pacing briefly to puff from his smoking pipe.

'The crime? Theft. The Criminal? Someone in this very room.'

'You can't suspect us, Detective, we're the ones who hired you,' argued the man with a bow tie.

'Indeed you were, Lord Melman - London's top Mayonnaise Connoisseur - but as the teens these days say: he who smelt it, dealt it. Who among you can say if you are truly innocent or not?'

'How dare you, sir?!' The summer hat-donned Lady spoke.

'That's the question, Lady Daffa - Liverpool's Teacake specialist - for how dare one of you feign ignorance as one of your acquaintances takes the fall for your crime,' Bane countered, taking another puff.

'Poppycock and balderdash!' exclaimed the man in hunter attire. 'I refuse to tolerate this tomfoolery anymore.'

'So you have expressed, Sir Crumpet - Owner of 'Game B&B' across West Yorkshire - when you willingly delayed my investigation with repeated attempts to leave the premises without authorisation, and blatantly refused to answer my questions. That too is a crime of its own.'

'Given the nature of the theft, I fail to see how I am suspect to scrutiny,' the second woman inquired as she adjusted her glasses.

'On the contrary, Miss Magniss - Science Teacher at Cambridge University - for one of your intellectual capacity would see this as a mental exercise to break the boredom, test the waters and thus prove your superiority.'

'You're good, Mr. Bane.'

The detective accepted the compliment as he allowed the group to settle.

'As I said, all within this room are suspects, and that includes our kind butler, George. No hard feelings,' Bane apologised, sipping the wine that George served.

'None at all, Sir,' replied George. 'We do what our job demands.'

'Too true, George.' A sip of wine to wet his whistle. '1989 vintage?'

'Yes sir, 1989 vintage from the Vineyard in Paris.'

'Paris, was it?'

'Southern district, if I recall.'

'Excellent year. Thank you, George.'

'You're welcome, sir.'

Another sip and a puff, and the Detective resumed his pacing.

'I'll admit that the crime itself had me quite stumped, at first. But I have heard the alibis, examined the scene, gathered the evidence and have identified the one who stole the great late Mona Mertyl's secret Quadruple Chocolate Brownie recipe.'

Everyone held their breath. Bane had their undivided attention.

'And the culprit is...'

All were silent. Who could it be?

'...blargh..'

Thud. Gasps.

George, closest at the time, moved towards the fallen detective and checked his pulse.

'Sir Bane is deceased,' he declared.

'Is it contagious?' asked Lady Daffa.

'Deceased, Ma'am, not diseased.'

'Between thievery and death, I've had enough,' exclaimed Lord Melman. 'I'm out.'

Melman reached for the door, but fell on his rear after he tried and failed to open it.

'The door's locked,' he cried. 'We're trapped!'

'By Foreman's Grill we are!' Sir Crumpet charged forward to break down the door; the Lord and Lady feebly joined the effort.

Miss Magniss, however, decided to finish what the late detective started and solve his last case. With the others occupied, she was left in peace to look over Bane's notes, pausing briefly to sip her glass of wine when George offered. The sharp taste helped to maintain her concentration.

George resolved to be silent until asked otherwise, for that was the role of a Butler.

Crumpet was losing patience and lifted the display axe from the wall; Melman and Daffa took a rapier each, and were ready to rip the door apart.

'Listen up, you lot.' Miss Magniss's voice caused the trio to stop their latest attempt.

'I may not be a detective, but I'm far from incompetent. Not only have I learned the thief's identity, I've also discovered the one responsible for Mr. Bane's predicament. That's right, murder is afoot.'

All but Miss Magniss gasped.

'Hear me well, for I will reveal the true culprits, right

now!'

All were silent.

Thud. Screams.

George, once more, was the one who checked for a pulse.

'Miss Magniss is decea- *ahem* -dead.'

'Don't panic, people,' Lord Melman panicked. 'If we think about this logically--'

'Forget logic, man!' Sir Crumpet yelled. 'Anyone who's ever read a mystery novel knows exactly who's behind it all: The Butler!'

'Of course, the Butler did it,' Lady Daffa agreed. 'He poisoned the wine.'

'That is both cliché and preposterous,' George defended. 'Slander stemming from Mary R. Rinehart's 'The Door'. She never even used the line.'

'He didn't deny the crime, did he?' Sir Crumpet noted.

'Apprehend him!' ordered Lady Daffa.

The trio backed George against the wall, until the window behind him broke and he fell to the jagged rocks in the sea below: a glimpse of red all that was seen.

'Does anyone else fail to see the logic of having a house built on a precarious cliff over the raging sea?' Lord Melman asked.

'We abandoned logic, remember?' Sir Crumpet stated.

'Right, right. Apologies.'

'Hold on, boys,' Lady Daffa interjected. 'Abandoning logic doesn't mean that we have become stupid. We ate the same meals and drank the same wine, so if the Butler really did it, then wouldn't we all be dead right now?'

They thought silently about it for some time.

Thud. Thud. Thud.

The clock tolled three. All were dead.

Buzz! Buzz! Buzz!

The body of Detective Bane sat up suddenly; he fuddled

about until he pulled out a small phone from his inside coat pocket, vibrating in his hand.

'They call that a 'gentle' wake up call? But it worked, as did the fake death and revival pills,' he said aloud, feeling around his mouth with his tongue. 'Flavours could be improved, though.'

Bane stood up, dusted himself off and examined the scene before him until his eyes spied his spilt glass. 'Shame, that was a rare vintage, too,' he sighed, then spotted the broken window and the torn tuxedo fabric on the glass shard.

'Poor George. He never got to enjoy his Mother's brownies after all.' His gaze turned to the four dead bodies. 'Still, credit where it's due, the man had great tastes in wine. It complimented the Iocane Powder rather nicely. Pity he didn't know I had built up an immunity to it, work hazards and all. That said, it gave me the perfect opportunity to follow through with my plans.'

As he spoke, Bane had removed his work clothes and re-dressed himself with the contents of a bag that he'd hidden beneath the dining table.

'With that, my last case is complete and my retirement begins. Good-bye, Detective Bane.' He put on his blonde wig before stepping in front of the nearest body mirror to tidy himself up, dress and all, 'Hello, Dorothy Cane!'

After one surprisingly fluid sashay through the mansion, Dorothy kicked the front door open and jumped down the step in an almost glide.

She hopped on her reliable motorcycle, side saddle, as lady-like as possible, revved up and rode on towards the sunset.

After all was said and done, Dorothy was finally free to follow the steps of his great role model, Berwick Kaler, and become the next Great Dame of Pantomime.

# Walking

## Keith V. Myers

Meeting my new friend Rachel
near the river
Where the boats go by
Bob is my name
My dog Peter the retriever
will accompany me
We meet on a bench and chat
Both in our twenties
So it's mobiles and games
Everyday things
Running, keeping fit
As we walk, Pete looks at Rachel
to give him a stroke
Bob gives her a peck on the cheek
A boat passes, rippling the water
people wave
We wave back, say what a nice day
Passing over , we meet different people
Pete plays with other retrievers
The ducks and geese waddle about
But there's a shout
Teams of rowers racing each other
Local rivalry involved.

As we sit on a seat, we spot the ice cream boat
Bob gets two cones
we enjoy a sit and suck
We walk to the park, see the squirrels, doves and robins
People relaxing on the grass

Chatting away
Taking in every word.

We saunter
    and come across eagles,
Who can perch on your arm
'For a small fee you can take a picture of me'
Wandering
    we see young people, couples and the elderly
Walking, talking
Taking in the views.
Another ice cream venue,
    beware of the queues
Leaving the park we agree
What a lovely time we have had.

Let's do it again some time soon.

# Sunset Abyss on the Evening Sea
# The Two One Once

## TNX

Out, to the west, through the valleys and past the surrounding mountain tops, tucked within a circular wall of rock faces, sits a cove, one like no other. Atop the hardened, weathered perimeter exuberant meadows extend beyond the focus of one's eye. Rich in wild plant-life and constantly animated by a vast array of creatures in all shapes and sizes, the location is the truest depiction of a natural paradise.

Nestled in the cradle of the cove, hundreds of feet above the bleached sands, a serene lake lays in-wait, fed by seven separate streams stretching down from each mountainside village, all seven currents are said to symbolise a different key human emotion. The lake acting as a cauldron melds these streams into one body of liquid, eternally brimming with the essence of life. The fresh mineral waters inundate their confines, pushing themselves over the edge, in doing so creating an ever-flowing, crystal-clear waterfall that cascades off the cliff down to the tip of the ocean below. From its vaporous breath a mist runs rampant, dictating the environment's humidity, allowing every surface to glisten, and every ray of light to hum and bellow upon the ground below, painting the world as it so chooses. Directly across from the waterfall, meticulously positioned due west and preventing a perfect circumference, the cove's narrow mouth maintains the light until it is swallowed by the ocean's nightly appetite. Once a circumsolar cycle, weather-permitting, an astrological alignment buries the star into the depths precisely betwixt the near-monolithic imposing walls of the cove's jaws. This otherworldly event creates a unique natural phenomenon; illuminating the cove in its descent the Sun's light travels the full spectrum as it plucks at the waves, embodies the mist and strokes each surface before darkness claims the

land. Throughout the closing hours of the evening the bay lives through every hue imaginable, tricking both the flora's and the fauna's grip on reality as it simulates each season in rapid succession.
The townsfolk in the surrounding lands regard it as a deeply spiritual experience, one that allows, for a brief spell, the heavens to communicate with the denizens that have wilfully settled upon the awkward angles of the mountainous cusp's enclosure. This has led to many a pilgrimage from worlds well beyond view, even as far as shores where limitations in language have left locals of the cove to assume the unmapped nations remain nameless. All hoping to witness these splendorous delights.
It is, in short, a spectacle that summarises all life, a timeless window into evolution's plans: the ultimate sunset.
But with such an abundance of divine traits must come a contrast, an element that prevents the area from being too welcoming: a necessary danger. After all, everything must protect itself to some degree.
Unfortunately, given the extremities to all senses on show, the event has proven time and time again to fracture even the strongest of minds. The overwhelming nature of the occurrence has proven too much for the vast majority of visitors, the weight of the motions buckling brains under the pressure of its sheer magnitude. Countless bodies drop from the cliffs, wash up on the shore, bury themselves to hide from their madness, or some simply disappear, traceless.
The only souls to surpass this taster of nirvana are those in the company of their true soulmate. It is the unparalleled test to recognise the required balance of an essential stabling figure. One should only ever build their future after establishing the most important of foundation blocks. As such, the few that dare to take the risk are most often lonely dreamers, desperate to encounter their ideal other…

*Deep Blue*

*One ocean, curtailed at the horizon by it's bodiless, brighter overseer,*
*One sky, with its back to a world petrified in its shaded wake,*
*An eternity of empty glaring, never a second spent sharing,*
*A mass of entirety in all directions, life's insignificance the only relevance,*
*Sharp waves, cursed winds, as heavens open, the tears begin,*
*Too wet to hold, too stubborn and old, all only cold,*
*Life is alone.*

Broken by solitude.
Haunted by past love.
Nervously, he approaches.
Quietly, she waits, in hope.
His frown cuts through harsh winds.
Settled is she, within the soft clasp of a willow tree.
Dishevelled, he irons out unfamiliarity with a clammy palm.
Hidden by branches, she echoes each thought into her journal.
The pages of his history are ripped and frayed.
Whereas, the pictures from hers are colourless and faded.
An uncharacteristic step into a world where he holds no map.
One last push for a dream in reality, else a return to the ghosts that suffocate.
Land not his friend, finally the trial uphill comes to an end.
Her eyes pull away from the page as an air of change frees her locks.
Beyond his weather-battered demeanour a vibrant meadow greets him.
Her focus drawn to beyond the wooden bars of her chosen cell.
Ahead lies a tree, with him in need of shelter and warmth.
A silhouette emerges upon the leaves, a guest has arrived.
Futures apart, awaiting a crack in the shell of a willow tree.

*Violet*
*Life's answers give wings to further questions,*
*Streams shiver under their own weight, fuelled by the short life of snow on slate,*
*Sights unseen unearthed from birth, a new world awakes nearing the firth,*
*The morning wail of the mourning whale, its ripples and spray conceal circling osprey,*
*No path is ever walked twice, no two waters make the same ice,*
*A day's rhythm starts alone, lyrics unpredictable kept unknown,*
*No creature holds a word of a song unheard.*

Sensing respite he waves nature's curtain aside.
Through the leaves a worn hand steps forth inside.
His eyes surprised, he uncovers the tree's most captivating flower.
Protecting her habitat, juggling caution with optimism, never to cower.
Lost for words he attempts a smile — a forgotten victim thought drowned.
No stranger to imposing advances, her body, brave, holds ground.
Recognising a mismatch in class, his arms fold, hiding his past.
Eagle-like she spies scars from hooks and teeth, an incomplete tale of ink beneath.
He looks beyond her glasses; skin like snow, home-made clothes, rough jewellery.
Is it a scowl or squinted grin, she asks within, studying his tan, the lines therein.
Though her figure seems slender, it speaks more of a life not kind or tender.
Trying not to judge her gaze wanders his attire; just a man, only a man.
Calming, his stance slumps, courteously he sits, letting the breeze run between.
Easing, she permits his share of the shade, soothed by his lack of demands made.

The air brings him his first scent; lavender hiding a musky hint of stagnation.

A taste of sea salt hits her lips, followed by a rare empty air of a man unloved.

Gravelly and unpractised, he commits, 'Be all well?'

Appreciative of his measured approach she smiles, 'All be well'.

Their many differences no more any different.

*Green*

*Cocooned in fresh reeds the swan's neck cranes,*
*Peering out, it yearns a reflection but not one mirrored in the lake,*
*Plant stems holding no flower bounce and shake over blades that shimmer,*
*Frogs capture lily-pads, squirrels await signs of ripening, the motion field mice bring,*
*Cattle graze with an eye raised, bushes flutter housing chirps that stutter,*
*Break-time in the seaweed but classmates stay in study,*
*And the swan sees all, still, too timid to call.*

'The constant sway of the tide... and now such stillness'

'From daylight hours I regretfully hide... this place 'can cure a heart's illness''

'Be that at the risk of a man's mind'

'And there no place for a lady's pride?'

'We all have trod a different path, yet only you and I appear to the world as lost'

'Or, perhaps we are the only ones to find it? All roads inevitably cross'

He turns his head, the winds whisk, her hair dark and alive takes his eyes.

As she tames her mane she peeks out and briefly meets his gaze.

Unprepared and coyly lent he looks ahead, fearful for the time already spent.

'No waiting 'widow' from the shore you left abandoned?'
She bites playfully.
Slighted by shock he chuckles, 'Only the sea, no other awaits my return'
'So were you to slip and return, without pulse, no inquest would ever learn?'
His face cracks, a smile arrives, 'I see why you sit alone, on nature's finest throne'
A relief washes over her, 'Life is too complex to worry about what's next'
'The only wasted minutes are ones spent wishing for a perfect second'
'Allow the heart some wants, won't you? Though not insatiable, it does hunger?'
'Of course', the hairs on his neck tremble, '...Why else would I sit here?'
'Other than sea legs and a spume mind, I guess it is possible for your kind...'
Expectations left unshattered will refuse to build anything that matters.

*Yellow*

*Rising squid spin under the spotlight, saluting compass corners past sight,*
*Waters erupt, tribulation simmers, turbulence camouflaging untold finned swimmers,*
*Slick shags and salty cormorants slap splash in ways of whimsy,*
*The bee stays gleeful to secure its own desires, spreading seeds of glory,*
*The gluttons of glow, dandelions, lounge for their nourishment on show,*
*Chemicals change, a joyous range, others now no longer strange,*
*Heavens embrace, leaving no cold shoulder in this place.*

'You never let the waves take your hand? Or do you stall, foot in sand?'
'A woman petrified? By water? We're no longer the working man's daughter'

'My pardons please beg, company is bereft, so too being still of leg'
'At least you back down, unlike the suits I have around' she plucks petals.
He leans to her side, 'That flower cause you some harm?'
'No. But it's beauty causes me some alarm' she places it back down.
He picks it up, inspecting it, 'To take such beauty, is that not too cruel?'
'Perhaps... but too much appeal and the wrong audience expects a feel'
Carefully placing it back down, 'Grey roses safer than red?'
'Aesthetics are semantics, painted and patterned, the rose is still a rose in its bed'
'...Rich in palette, alive in every way, the cold rock face sees all, enlivened by day'
'A man who wakes to the sound of seagulls dropping dinner, this place is bliss?'
A cushioned chuckle escapes his grasp, 'The cold rock face ain't the landscape...'
Briefly offended only to upend it, 'Hm, a witty man from water... a welcome *catch*'
Noticing a warmth in her teasing snarl he moves ever so slightly her way.
Pretending not to notice his slight approach, her body feigns a damsel in the wind.
Removing his jacket, he neatly folds the lifeless skin and hands it across.
She inspects it, surprisingly clean, 'Thank you... will fetch a good penny at market'
The shell shed, truths said, comfort found, in one another's head.

*Orange*

*Feet relentless living restless, dancing on warming crumbs of yesterday,*
*Eliminated are those who toy for fun, there remains a competition to be won,*

*Threats arrive in land, sea and air, games no longer fair,*
*Four eyes on two, bone and antler clash until dust and ash,*
*The Earth's fingers' skin does anxiously shed, pressing down on tired, wilted beds,*
*Fissures pressured on edges up high, land gives way, the face beneath stays shy,*
*All enter with renewed purpose, trust comes hard in the inescapable furnace.*

The winding pathways of a special chemistry unchartered, happiness bartered.
A familiar loss of intrigue lands, her focus returns to her lap holding itchy hands.
Aware his self unaware, unremarkable on a crowded shelf, why would she reach?
Eclipsed by hanging bitterness, and a fear of being found again, would he seek?
His lips move to mould a word, instead drops a mumble barely heard.
Fixed on his broken speech, she fails to hear... was it meant for another's ear?
Unsettled by her sigh and turn of thigh, he surmises he must be the wrong guy.
Was her skin too pale, frame too frail, too indoorsy for a man who sets sail?
A rare miscalculation, drenched in choppy waters, with no worthy bait, clutching only salt.
Again, again, again, her life spins, crowds disperse, and alone again she halts.
Fearing turning her taste further away, he walks to the edge, overlooking the bay.
Jilted? Sat past his shadow, downtrodden, yet enamoured by his outline glow.
Now regretting his cold relocation, from a pocket he drops a hand, it waits patient.
Is he too just a bumbling fool? Two of a kind, both loving but insecure of mind.
Years of bites but yet one that excites, he frees his fingers to fish in the light.

Getting up she sees man in a different form, honest as earth, complex and torn.
His hands be shovels, lonely icicle-like digits cry down, entombing hers three fold.
Hers elegant like wands, pluck up the courage to fill in the gaps… then take hold.
The chaos of doubt at last arrested, insecurities both downed and bested.

*Red*
*Veins spread, cheeks blush, in the head, a dizzying rush,*
*The face of yesterday pushed aside, shoots of new life in each pride,*
*The world's walls wear a new mask, heartstrings pull at a new task,*
*Vines entwine, between wing beaks sing, resting deer ear-on-ear,*
*Nature's ark pairs up all souls, today the last test of a life now old,*
*Murmurations, constellations, the skies bleed fascination,*
*Every memory shared a vital piece of a life better spent paired.*

Relaxed and no longer a fist, her heartbeat rests safe in his leathery net.
His skin rough, her fingers grip tight, purpose delivered, finally, a new night.
Their lives seem unalike in simple form, attending different sides of the same storm.
Though his appearance akin to granite, a crack is found where her heart may sit.
Witnessing the same fears brought by unrelated years, he cherishes such a bond.
Now leaning on his arm, pulse humming, she only wants now, no past or beyond.
A bodily calm, never found before, he stands content but… does she desire more?
Frightened of change, to wake from this dream, she prays frost consume the scene.
Sunsets on the sea, to him, simply normalcy, but this…

Nights under the tree, to her, merely deflect tragedy, but this…

The day's light approaching submerged, a torch's last dance, his chance soon purged.

Time the enemy of tranquillity, she begs to the sky to let sleeping dogs lie.

Should he swoon her, sweeping her up? Or would brash masculinity turn her off?

Rushed she desperately plots her next move, watching on as shadows creep forth.

He looks for the words but only finds rust.

She whets her lips but only brings dust.

Travelling through rocky shores his words moor, 'This is everything…'

Running down off the sands her lips quiver, '…All I've ever wanted'.

The match struck, sparks ignite, their tongues roll off the cliffs their cheeks climb.

*Indigo*

*The final flickers of light's shift rest on a current set adrift,*
*Sheltered from imminent frost, the creatures seem long lost,*
*The flowers swaddle themselves, not knowing if they'll wake,*
*With tired skin the clouds thin, streams cease along with belief,*
*Earth is closed to guests,*
*The spectacle beatless in its chest,*
*The body is gone, and it wants nothing left.*

His story's markings turn sore, earned from the jaws of daily war.

Her thoughts return from the darkness, skittishly firing, in need of a harness.

A bewildering sense of recompense pushed aside, his demons he can no longer hide.

Unravelled her hectic mind rolls, are they not aligned, these two souls?

The tales were true, madness in view, his body quick to tense, this be the expense.

Like fake pearls embarrassing beads trickle down, hope lost she longs to drown.
All beauty near washed away, his sight stolen, compass amiss, life is no gift.
Her smile frayed, complexion flayed, the land not delivered for what she prayed.
Everything fizzles to naught, emptiness caught.
Her bearings in disarray, only feeling dismay.
Thoughts blacken, sanity slackens.
Hopes crushed; men are not to trust.
Empty. Enraged. A beast, uncaged.
Suspicious. Unstable. A wicked fable.
A gritted smirk, he grows berserk.
A pen she grabs, the pages she stabs.
He turns to her, no longer him…
She looks at him, no heart therein…
The moment passed, sanity now glass, plunging down, soon to crash.

*Black/White*

*Black, the night takes hold, the Moon too weak, no day to mould,*
*All disappears, sound sinks, taste dissipates, aroma abandons,*
*If only for the night, existence dies…*
*In the far corner of nothing, a hope starts swelling,*
*Space sends a beacon, the night senses treason,*
*Tiny mouths applaud, paths shake, plants rise, alive again overflows the lake,*
*Across the stratosphere from on far, all captured by a shooting star,*
*A night sky everything will remember, darkness defeated, by a single ember.*

In the flash night briefly breaks, his mind returns, his senses rewake.
Scattered scribbles of thoughts lift, clarity the evening's final gift.
The Earth has granted approval, an opportunity awarded, in a glance.

With heavens' blessing, a window opens; their last chance.
Looking ahead his heart desperately sets a new course.
Reaching up, all faith in-tow, pushed by an unwavering force.
Her eyes take his.
His hands take hers.
The meeting of lips.
Tangling finger tips.
Fleshes mingle, nerves tingle, ducts tear, overcoming fear.
They connect.
Their auras blend.
Their scars heal.
Their hearts ascend.
In the journal they begin to write, in ink, in blood, they unite…

*Deep Blue*
*The Sun retires back to all seas' bed,*
*The birds breathless, nothing left to be said,*
*Waters cool, fish go back to school, and the waves settle,*
*Bees on their knees, butterflies lie, now only moonlight caresses the petal,*
*All hunger thwarted, all deeds done, tomorrow's seedlings now all begun,*
*He cradles her, she breathes in him,*
*Neither with regret, watching stars bury their first sunset…*

*Life is all one.*

# Against the clock

## Samantha Martin

The sound of silence is elusive
I seek its comforting weight...
... it soothes me

Sometimes
It catches me quick, by surprise
My ears
They s i g h
and they s o f t e n....
..
From the din and the clamouring
The chaos, the yammering
The bangs and the clattering
Next door and her chattering
The dog who is scattering
The pigeons that flap at him
The postman rat tat ting
Old Joe lets his cat in
The work calls, the zoom calls
Non stop as the rain falls
On the shed with the red roof
Grab lunch on the hoof
Kids leaving school

Acting the fool
Playing it cool
Up there in the park

Until...
Until it gets dark
Silence
it gladdens my heart, it resets my rhythms

And now? Now I can start..

# Pomegranate

## Nicky Kippax

You
are never alone
when eating a pomegranate
all those pithy layers unfold to expose
tender pink gems in ivory gums - snapping
apart under the pull of your palms - big reveal -
if only you're bold enough to twist the tough husk
set loose the companionship of translucent jewels
if only you're bold enough to twist the tough husk
apart under the pull of your palms - big reveal -
tender pink gems in ivory gums - snapping
all those pithy layers unfold to expose
when eating a pomegranate
you are never ever
alone.

# Dancing 'till Dawn

## Elaine Kelly

Yesterday whispered a truth to me:
*'It won't last'*.

I didn't believe it, why would I? Why would I want to believe it? You see, yesterday tasted like sunshine. It tingled and sparkled and held me with a tenderness that reached my very soul. I danced in the light that shone all around me. I swirled so fast it was easy to ignore those words in the corner,

*'It won't last'*.

'MEMENTO MORI!' twirl, whirl, unfurl myself completely in its song. I didn't notice the music change - I just danced in time with each new melody. I only wanted to hear that tune, as long as it played, I spun and swayed. I didn't listen to the words,

'It won't last.'

The day it stopped I heard new words:

*'It's over!'*

I kept moving, I grasped at wisps of sound, but the melody was gone. My limbs grew heavy and slow. The light ebbed away. The silence shattered my being. I lumbered through the solitude. Where is the music to keep me warm? Yesterday had told me a truth. I almost retched at the bitterness of my acceptance.

But then a moment approached and whispered to me
*'Stop (...)'*.
I brushed it away. It came again

'(...) *Listen (...)*'.
I shook my head to make it go.

## *'Stop, listen, look!'*

The moment held me; I didn't resist. I raised myself up. A creeping recognition allowed me to see. Fatigue dripped away and there it was. The day, today, in full motion. My heart in rhythm, with a gentle song, ticked along to the beat of time, faces filled with life moved around me. Clouds meandered in the sky.

Then I felt the wind, a mother wind, it moved through my hair and caressed my skin.

# Pain

## Carol Coffey

I'm sure I'm addicted to pain. I know the word well, I know the dangers and warning signs. The fear of it - dragging - but yet I simply can't swim away from it, like that waterfall coming up, that volcano erupting in front of you, the sun we aren't meant to look at. It's impossible to look the other way.

I crawl, roll, fall, whatever's the quickest way to it. It always finds me. People say why go to the gym, why do that? I think, WHY? I don't know why, but I'm never going to stop.

The fire - it has me in the heat, the tiger in its claws, that boy who had you in those muscles, that last drink you simply couldn't avoid.

I can't hide - it knows all the hiding spots, like that worst boyfriend you just simply couldn't shake off, that cold that lingered, that teacher who just wouldn't quit. You know what I mean - pain, like mud, sticks. Like the police - you only speed up one minute, next you're on that driver awareness course. Then the pain of the course - losing hours of your day - but actually you really enjoy it and learn things. You have to pay for it, but it hooks you in.

The frame, the wheelchair, the equipment, the Motability car - but you then just do more and more. Fill life even more. I'm addicted. All the Personal Independence Payment appeals, but you carry on - just another fall, more appointments, more scares.

Oh, how I'm addicted to pain - it's my friend no matter what, it quenches a thirst.

Now everyone will want my friend, pain. It's very loyal - in fact it could teach a dog a thing or two - and dogs don't miss a thing: you sat on the loo or sound asleep in your bed.

Pain is my best friend and I never asked it to be my friend - but it won't leave me alone. No matter how much I kick it. It's like playing chess with Sam or Roy or even escaping that devil Stephen in *Coronation Street* - just not possible.

I defy its orders - challenge, rebel, fight, ignore - but I have more control over resisting chocolate.

Pain, how I so hate you. But you do make my life interesting, to say the least.

One night, you might think the pain has gone, but little did you know it is on a sleepover so - shit - no sleep!

# A Cacophony of Thoughts

## Bekhi Ostrowska

**Cascading**
**Crawling**
**Creeping**
**Colliding**
**Charging**
**Catapulting**
**Crashing**
**Contorting**

**Cascading** through cornfields
**Crawling** through meadows
**Creeping** into pastures
**Colliding** into tree trunks
**Charging** through woodlands
**Catapulting** into haystacks
**Crashing** through forests
**Contorting** past glades

**Cascading** through cornfields – Being pricked by sharp stalks
**Crawling** through meadows – Confused evening walks
**Creeping** into pastures – Trying not to look back
**Colliding** into tree trunks – As I run from the pack
**Charging** through woodlands - Outrunning blind fear
**Catapulting** into haystacks – Leap makes it clear
**Crashing** through forests – Dreams are shattered
**Contorting** past glades – Words never mattered

Sharp stalks **cascading** my mind
Evening walks **crawling** to find
Look back whilst **creeping** around
The pack **colliding** through sound
Blind fear is **charging** my being
Clear its **catapulting** my seeing
Shattered shards **crashing** to earth
Never mattered **contorting** my worth

**Cascading** waters surround me
**Crawling** over moss laden rocks
**Crawling** towards a mouth that is open
**Colliding** with stones taking knocks
**Charging** my once empty batteries
**Catapulting** the strength that is real
**Crashing** down barriers meant to block
**Contorting** the heart-break I feel

# I know I let you down and said the wrong thing

## Chad Copley

*Chad's side* *His friend's side*

You are my state of mind
My victory, my choice, my destination
You resonate in my decisions and choices
You help me to understand my mind's voices
And help me heal.

My love
what do you know of my state of mind
and what matters to me?
You defy me and give me indecision
And my hopes and fears evolve around your choices.
And you love and adore me and I loved you for it.
You bring calmness but I need to fulfil my dreams
You are aware of me and my family.
I will not surrender myself - indeed I will not
You punish me with insecurity
and I want you to walk away so we can heal

Please come back and stay
and scare the darkness away.
You are what I identify with
and what I want.

I will not come back and stay
and scare your woes and fears away.
Your perpetual darkness is of your own making.
You are not what I want at the moment.

Why are you not there?
You seem not to care -
you don't ring
you refuse to see me.
Why me? Why me?
This can't be happening to me.

I need you not to fuss
I will be there when I am good and ready.
I believe you could break my fall.
Please help, please help
give me time my love

If you ring, I will be there
and hold your hand.
And together we will make a stand
to fight the competitive, nasty and negative.
I know I let you down and said the wrong thing.

# Snap, Crack, Wallop

## Christina O'Reilly

I hear a flitter flutter, a flighty humming of wings; a wave of cool air rolls across my arms, face and chest. I shiver, quiver, as I'm forced out of a deep sleep.

Coming out of a wonderful dream, I notice light but not ordinary light, small fluffy fuzzy, my eyelids are being pulled open; I jump, sit up, so fast my head spins, I'm going lefty, righty, flipping, flopping, backwards, forwards like a jack in the box, I try to reach for the light, a small object moves in the darkness towards me. I'm still shocked and sleepy, the feeling of sickness like a boat in rough sea but, nope, I've definitely got my hand out towards the lamp, I've stopped dead in my tracks, it's still moving towards me in the darkness; I hear a tinkle, jingle, chime of bells, now slowly it starts to glow.

To my amazement, the most beautiful pair of opal wings are opening in front of me, bright white with reds, greens, blue, orange swirling, twirling, eddying in a different direction.

It's looking at me, I think it's trying to smile; it's more like a grimace, I can't contain my shock and slide back; to my surprise there's a snap, crack, wallop and thwack —

I'm falling back. I look at my arm which is hurting shuddering, juddering, glowing, growing, like a caricature of an inflatable lilo floating in a swimming pool; suddenly all goes black.

I come to, feeling as if I've been hit by a bolt of energy; not the nice vim and vigour energy you have after you've been to the gym, but like I've walked into an electric fence or was hit with a cattle prod; frozen in one position, everything hurts.

I'm seeing triple evil pixies. In my mind fairies are very different: they don't hurt people on purpose, are kind and humanly beautiful. 'What am I saying?'

Heart racing, head thumping, tears flowing, I manage to turn my head left, there's my arm floating above my head. I turn back there's still three pixies; the other two have the same body, different wings, just as beautiful.

The second one has the head of a dragon fly, wings of emerald green with lime, jade, forest greens (the Island of Dr Moreau comes to mind). The other is more like a sunny autumn day, wings of reds, rusts, golds: their wings are just a profusion of colour.

Opal, its teeth - well fangs to you and me – are protruding; it's kind of grim really. I think it's saying, 'Oops sorry.'

Suddenly, there's a sound like a dog with a squeaky toy or three dogs with squeaky toys. I lean forward slowly to see if I can understand them; I don't know which one noticed, again with the snap, crack, wallop and thwack, I'm falling back this time the pains on the right side of my face already I can't see out of my eye, the side of my face is swelling, bulging, distending like an over ripe tomato withered, wrinkled, wasted and crinkled, skin drying out about to split, innards' seeping slowly out.

Pain shudders through my face and arm, I can't lift my head, all I see is a tumbling, lurching, shimmering, and flickering of colour, the pixies are fighting again but have wrapped themselves into a ball. It reminds me of a disco ball. I haven't seen those colours before, weird, fading out...

I come back, hoping it's been a dream. I try to sit, but the left hand side of my face feels heavy, the right hand side feels light and floaty like my arm, and there's something glowing above me.

I have no movement. I think it's fear, I want to be sick. 'Am I dying?' I ask out loud. No one hears. Tears start to roll down my face, but somehow on the right hand side of my face they don't seem to fall, puddling in the swollen grooves which makes me cry more.

I wish I could wake up from this terrifying nightmare. I try to control my breathing, in for five, out for ten; if you do yoga you'll know this is a calming exercise for slowing everything down and oxygenating the blood.

In my fuddled mind I'm trying to do a few tai chi moves; it feels like I'm underwater, slow motion big, big over the top movements; my body seem to be like a blimp, I'm parting the horse's mane, repulsing the monkey and a single whip trying to protect myself. Huge sobs shuddering through my prostrate body. I really don't understand.

Arm like a lilo, head resembling a large hideous tomato I'm also thinking about how long this seems to have been going on.

I hear the bells from before but there are more of them, bigger, louder: this time I really feel I'm going to die in my sleep; heart and head pounding, a pulsating in my ears, temples on one side twitching. Above me, bigger than the three little pixies, a shape the size of a small child is heading towards me, face to face, an adult, I think. Its wings are blackened like coal, every colour you know and more rolling like the night sky, like the cosmos you see in films (Star Trek comes to mind). Its body has a fuzzy skin, similar to a peach. 'What am I saying?'

Maybe call this one Cosmos? It seems to be carrying an older version of itself. Its wings are like shrivelling dry autumn leaves, but still so colourful - maybe an elder…

'What the hell do I know?' I say.

I hear a noise like glass, shingle, stones and hard core all in a cement mixer without water but, somehow, I understand it. It has an almost rhythmic beat to it, like an old fashioned tumble dryer, rum tum, rum tum, rum tum, it's saying I am coming with them, I will be taken to their home, I try to shout, 'No, I just want to wake up, this nightmare has gone on long enough thank you.' They're not looking at me.

I hear small bells; I look and see three little pixies hiding at the top of my curtains. The larger pixie turns sharply; they hide. I see the curtains shaking (I'm glad they're scared like me); I look up the bigger one (teeth huge); it looks at the older one who nods: and yes you guessed it snap, crack, wallop and thwack but I'm already on my back.

I wake I feel warm. I'm wrapped in my quilt even my head is cocooned, my arm still floating next to me, I can still only look up. We seem to be travelling through a vortex of swelling colour: sometimes I think I see trees, the moon, stars, I hear an owl, a scurrying sound of animals. I'm so sleepy, but I let out a sort of whimper simper sound, then Cosmos, the dark pixie, rolls over to face me. I didn't even realise it was at my side. I get a brief glance of black and gold stipes (reminds me of Dennis the Menace's jumper) as it rolls over; the small one asks - well more acts - a shivered, shake and patting itself with paws, for there are not hands. It's asking if I'm cold. I shake my head. 'No,' I squeak.

I now seem to be the same size as them, which is quite disconcerting. I hear a hiss from the elder, then a spider drops down on me. I scream - at least that's what I think I'm doing - it's started to spin me in it legs, spewing web out.

I smell honey, I feel a warm breeze on my face. At last my nightmare's finally over. I'm home in my bed, toast with honey for breakfast. Who's cooking it for me? I wonder, as I sigh with relief. Alas, as I open my eyes, Cosmos is looking down at me (I believe I see relief on its face) honey is dribbling from its mouth into mine. I gag, gag again but swallow.

I hear a grunt, a lot of scurrying then silence. It's still looking at me, I blink, I blink again; yes at last I can move my face. I smile. Cosmos flutters away a bit then returns over me. The grimace returns. I'm hoping it's a smile.

I look to my left; to my disappointment my arm's still floating; it's looking smaller but bruised and battered. I feel a sadness, tears fill my eyes, a hairy paw touches my face. I fall asleep before I can see who touched me.

Time has no meaning. Day, night, I have no idea how long this has gone on for: fed honey sleep repeat. I wake, I look round trying to clear my vision, I lift my arm. It's normal. I sigh.

I'm in a large hole. I can't see the top, it's endless. I feel cold, chilly, I wrap my arms round me; there's a drink next to me with some honey on a small piece of wood, the smell of earth is overwhelming, like it's just been dug. I realise it's a hollow, small glowing lights spinning around.

I pull myself up, turn on the spot, noting the sound of a low chant, bells, lots of bells, a sort of song, squeaky dog toys, cement mixer, the tinkle broken glass, it has a similar rhythmic beat to the sound I heard before, 'rum tum, rum tum, rum tum' from all corners, different insects of all shapes and sizes, pixies, small animals chanting to the same beat, the elder comes towards me all gravel and hard core voice: 'We are sorry, our young ones were playing a prank on each other, is how you say?'

'Yes,' I say, 'they followed an insect into—'

... a wave of its paw

I say, 'My home.'

'Yes,' the elder says.

I ask, 'Who are you?'

It says, 'I cannot know.'

I ask, 'Can I stay and learn from you?'

The paw goes in the air again: 'You cannot.'

I feel weird, the beat of the chanting going through me.

The elder speaks again, 'Our small ones wish to…' The pixie turns a paw in air; the three little ones fly forward, knocking into each other, wanting to be first. A massive 'hissssssssssssss' echoes through the hollow. The elder has stopped them in their tracks.

Slowly they move forward: Opal first, dropping a leaf-wrapped gift. I bend to pick it up, hold it in my hand worried it will blow up, a trick maybe - all this started with this one. The other two do the same; we stand there, their heads dipping like nodding dogs. I realise they want me to open their gifts.

One is a beautiful white wrap, like lace with a sticky consistency. The grimace on Opal's face makes me smile (I'm sure it's had it made from a spiders web). The second one is a dirty green emerald – no, crystal, maybe. I rub it and the swirling colours inside remind me of its wings. The third seems to be a rug of woven flowers, leaves, wool (I think) and feathers, all things from the woodland. I'm so touched my eyes fill with tears.

I've been so frightened since this started, yet the only thing they've done is try to help. I feel slightly ashamed but fear's a funny old thing, and I wonder, 'Am I having an epiphany?'

Cosmos' wings are incredible; the colours seem to spin in a different way from the others. With a flit and a skim it comes forward, sets something else on the floor. It's a pouch. I pick it up.

I look; so does the elder. Cosmos shrugs its wings, making a sucking, wobbly sound like jelly being wiggled on a plate. I drop my gifts inside. The sound makes me giggle for the first time in a long time.

I'm happy. How funny. I giggle again; they look back at

me, and I shrug. Cosmos hisses; its wings ripple. I start to feel sleepy; my head droops, 'The drink,' I murmur, and the elder hisses, 'Yes'.

All the while the chanting has been growing, rhythm getting louder, it's vibrating through my body now. I have just enough time to say 'thank you'. Cosmos picks me up in its paws, flies me out of the hollow, up into the sky. I feel tiny, really tiny, then darkness.

I've not yet opened my eyes and I'm smelling honey. Trying to move my arm and head they're painful I open my left eye and realise the right-hand side of my face is on a plate I'm covered in honey and butter as I lift it my face feels distorted I look at my reflection in the screen of my laptop the light reflecting off my face.

A piece of toast falls, my face looks twisted, distorted. I take a breath, realising the honey has stuck my wrinkles together and the butter's making it look like an over ripe tomato, split innards everywhere.

My left arm's gone to sleep underneath me, pins and needles coursing the pain, I flex my fingers it really hurts, I laugh, not my normal laugh, it has a slight hysterical sound. It stops; I have tears rolling down my face, I can't tell you why. Maybe I'm sad my nightmare wasn't true.

Light's breaking through. I slowly go upstairs, shower and change. I wander downstairs again. Toast cooking, kettle's on. All my body parts are in working order, although my arm's sore with small bruises, my face red and puckered like a tomato. I rub them to get life back into them. I feel a lethargy hanging over me.

I go upstairs to make the bed, and walk towards the storage box (my uncle made it for me when I was a teenager 'for secrets' he said). It's at the end of my bed now containing bed sheets etc. There on the top is a leather pouch. I sit next to it shocked, disbelieving - could it really have happened?

I slip my finger into the pouch, lift the edge and there I can see the white wrap, now so soft and dry, the blanket full of colour, so many scents. I feel through the outside of the pouch there's a hard lump. I'm guessing the crystal. I'm smiling with relief. I'm not mad.

Each day I take them out of the box, wondering what's happened to the pixies. I walk round the local nature reserve, hoping to see a sign of them. In my mind it's become something wonderful, not a scary anymore. I don't think anyone would ever believe me. I sigh.

Months later, I hear a sound at the back door: a fluffy, puffy, scratchy sound. 'That bloody rose bush,' I mumble, 'must trim it back.' I open the door, shears in hand, and standing there is a figure all in black. It has its back to me. It looks furtive, I go to quickly to shut the door; it hisses; I look, I'm shocked - as it turns I see it's Cosmos. A wooden and silk frame is covering his eyes, its wings folded like a fine piece of origami into the shape of a jacket.

Cosmos lifts its wing slowly. 'We need your help,' the elder rasps. It looks really old, withered, sick. I look back at the elder and pull my door open...

But, that's a story for another time.

# Long Night

## Ellie King

The night draws down
The cold comes in
And here I'm trapped
inside my skin

Another night
I see ahead
Alone within
this fortress bed

For here be dragons
Here be wraiths
No guardian shall
before me place
a ring of safety
So here I lay
I have no god
I can not pray

The darkness lays
in front of me
The dreadful thoughts
weigh heavily

I hear and feel
but I can't see
the break of dawn
when I'll be free

And I can hardly
bear this pain
Alone, in fear
It comes again

I need to occupy my mind
My thoughts are cruel
They are not kind

At night my brain
is not my friend
Does someone have
an ear to lend?
Could I call you
so you can end
this broken record?
Let's pretend
that all is well
and I'm okay
until the sunlight
starts the day

I'll hear a blackbird
as he sings
and all the sounds
that morning brings
The dogs will bark
The children shout
But I'll stay here
I'll not go out

For daylight means
that I can sleep
I am safe now
I can keep
the ghosts and monsters
locked away
So here I am
and here I stay

# My Voice

## Dawn Skelton

*The noteworthy attentiveness, new opportunities, enlightened clearer pathways.*
*I challenge controversial questions, in a poetic story, optimistic in attitude.*
*I am a writer with artistic morals.*
*I engage in an inventory from my deep-rooted, growth.*
*I acknowledge and listen to my fundamental values, enabling gentle progression.*
*My journey, my energy, the highs the lows, the unexpected pressures…*

*The earthquake, in the honesty of the rumble in my own bias with weighty dilemmas…*
*The worry to fall, the fear of a crashing collapse.*
*I could contentedly sit on the rock by the creek at the end of the river forever more.*
*In finding my safe space, dare I risk exploring the valleys ahead?*
*I like my own company, now never alone beside nature's energy.*
*The concrete solid grounding holding me at the end of rowing up the untold river.*

*My need in written format as I embark on the next step of my journey …*
*Precious delivery, words true to me, I take a chance, gaining faith in myself.*
*The set of foundations in my spirit, my soul.*
*Primitive rants, primitive extracts from innocent shyness, joy and force.*
*The continuum of my story.*
*The escapism, the journey of self-recognition,*

*Be with me, my story in the next episode in my life, the essence in assertion,*
*In a declaration in the power in owning my voice.*

*I collaborate control, behind past chaos.*
*My determination comes from the roots of my underworld,*
*flowering, significant beauty, the blooming blossom.*
*The magnificence of expansive development.*

The terrain in my trek is unsteady at first.
I find pleasure in nature, the delight that I am no longer trapped in internal hesitations.
I do not need a palace of jewels; I have richness in communication.
I have found a voice beyond the jumping switch of fear in my mind.
The narrative story I share, deep, complexed, creative.

The power of visualisation, appreciation of creative escape, to lands where I am heard.
My voice, I proudly share, in healing not hiding in the mist, in mighty muteness.
The ability, advancing to move on in my lifespan.

In finding stillness in silence!
In tranquil serenity I watch the sunset, the softness, red, pink, peachy, pale blue.
Pigments and tints of the surround of the sky above…
The shades as daylight fades, shifting to the dusk before nightfall, approaching twilight.
An evening when a half-moon with only a single star is brightly shining, drawing me in…

I take a breath in the uplifting, singular dominance, the

becoming of the night.
The glitter, the flicker, the gleaming glow, the twinkle, a sky of diamonds.

The wonder of the universe, it holds me in sensory peaceful calm,
In the atmospheric moment, I am transfixed staring above.
My wondering mind of nature's surprise…
In the depths of my wonder, the ponder in the search for the meaning in life.
I find I individually search for my own meaning, purposeful goals, strengthened resilience…

My pursuit to where?
I attempt to stay rational as I dreamily drift in the unknown quest, I advance in excitement.
I try to keep up with myself, the brazened footsteps, confidently taken.
I jump into my senses, headfirst, thrilled in newfound aliveness.
My wakeful alertness, beyond the blur, awakened, overwhelmed by senses of the surround.
So much to uncover, the supremacy in my energy, strange, surreal, comfortably bizarre.
In facing my personal darkness, challenging my demons.
I find an announcement, as I break through borders.

The simmering pot that was overflowing with energy, my outlet now a voice to inspire.
In the slur and splurge of words articulating wisdom, points of sustained logic…
I am slowly finding a middle ground,

Periods of balance now
in my life.
The freedom of release is liberating, freedom in my creative writing brings self-healing.
At first 'Freedoms Journey', finding safe consistency from my life guides.
The followed flow in discovered maturity, flourishing, Independence in self-worth…

I curiously question the serendipities of life.
Mysterious coincidences a meeting place aiding opportunities in a communitive platform.
The universal direction in educational connection, keeping my energetic spirit alive…
I now explore the world ahead, no longer in fear, or dread…
I comfortably delve into an impending future…
I feel I belong; in recognition I am accepted for being real, for who I am.

'Me'.

My dreamy unique impression in my quirky personality on show.
I am proud I kept going when murky, mist lay ahead!
I in honour stand tall on the top of a hill, declaring, bellowing, roaring from my core…
In vocal movement I shout at the top of my lungs.
I am thankful to be
alive!

I stand at the top of the many hills; my pace is steady walking through the valleys.
The part in me wishing to roll down the hill, sideways in laughter, rolling somersaults.
This flashing childhood memory, more robust, more daring!

As an adult if I did this, I would probably break several limbs.

The playful imagination, to have some fun, breaking from my stroll.

stopping to talk to the hillside goats munching on grass.
Then the glare of the wild hare peeking from its burrow, our eyes connect…
The wilderness, its surround, I take time to look around, I notice nature like never before…
I see the mountains ahead in view, the varied invigorating weather beside me on my trek.
The power of the wind catches my breath.
The gushing wet droplets down my face from torrential rain.

Oh, my wondering mind…

I sing, I mutter, I laugh, I dance.
The times I leap over the steppingstones at speed…
The time I take shelter, when unable to cross rivers, in the dangerous currents.
The time to be still, under the trees when a storm, bursts out of the sky unexpectantly!

The time to recharge, reflections, questions?
My destination, ever changing, unplanned…

The doubts I face at the crossroads I come across, which route do I take?
Aware my roaming ramble will end, the enjoyment in the

limbo land I am in,
captivated in imagery, pleasure in escapism.
The place in my journey of finding who I am, the long to expand my nomadic presence.
The longing wish to communicate, my descriptive adventures.

The enthusing desires as I head to the townships,
The prospects to connect, in hope to engage in city life?
My direction, for a time proceeding alone, the time to get used to my new outlook to life.
The wish to map out my journey in writing, keeping hope in ambition.
The time needed to feel real, letting go of the fear of haunting flashes.
The singular trek to come into my own, fully dedicated,
Intimate security independently liberated.

The joy in my metaphorical fantasy when beaming sunlight fills the day,
The breaks in the trail, the exploration of hidden caves,
The explorer in me locating, unearthing the hidden finds in the nooks and crannies,
of the hilly valleys.

The pressures in prediction in my perfection, the need to get somewhere,
what is over the mountains - way in the distance?
The townships in view, closely nearby.
My merging moods, sadness that this part of my trek is ending, slight apprehension...

the eager elation to connect in urban links, hopes in creative union.

The dream to sit around a village campfire, sharing my story of my journey in the wilderness.
stories of loss
stories of pleasure in joyfulness.
stories of fact.
I feel ready to bond in community togetherness.

I reflect,
The recollective thrill in self-humour singing out of tune at the top of the hill,
The echo of my voice in the caves, laughter, varied melodies,
The moments I felt so carefree, truly letting go.

The power of language, beyond speech, the wish to share my recollection of unusual tales.
This is my story of healing:
ready to listen. Tell me yours?
dance with me, sing with me, rant with me in animated sensual satisfaction.
Share with me your minds gallery, be my companion in visual compassion.
I can be whoever I want to be, in the journey finding self-ownership.
Innocence in fantasy, the misty clouds, the Eerie pathways I walked through, in searching…

If I did cartwheels down a city street, then shouted my heightened song singing in depth…
The likelihood to be witnessed as eccentric or viewed as

'ma…d'.
The person who may applaud and cheer me on, whispering to me.

'Carry on'… You have this…'

The invite to cartwheel down the street with me, in the pleasure of fun in an open heart…

The wondering of the valleys gave me time to consider my moral ethics.
There will be times that I will have healthy debates in the rapport in relationships.
The escapist in my soul needing grounding.
The links in communication, bringing educational opportunities.
The creative mind showing my jumping voice.

I have departed the woodland, the forests and hills.
I find joy of engagement, my chosen tribes, in the coastal towns, cities, the countryside.

I observe and participate in liaison in the city, my writing in poetry in metaphors, to read.
I am encouraged to share my words, in written and vocal rhymes.
I am captivated, by the written words of others,
academic facts,
fictional and fantasy escape.
There is so much to take in, so much to learn in dazzling inspiration…

The rousing society that is beaten down in storms.
The angry ambience parts bringing a splash of sunshine, a surround of glorious weather.
The days with aimable goals, I thrive,
The days I feel exhausted, as the saying goes: 'walking

through treacle.'
The moody skies make me appreciate the hues of light amongst the shadow's silhouettes.
My watchful eye to society's culturally diverse blend.
The need to listen in empathic care to the town's folk in life's unfairness.

The seasonal pigments a healthy distraction, in the rush of the busy community.
The joy of new engagement…
The occasional pull to head back to a shelter of camouflage in the wilderness.
In awareness, the spectator in life, in the death of seasons of nature's earthly dynamic view.
The hidden finds, the encounter of a butterfly that crosses my eye, momentarily flashing by.
The grace of the flock of birds in flight, flying to continents new.

In community engagement, full speed ahead,
The importance of sharing endearing moments, a leader in connection.
I am the director in boundaries, the protective controller.
The disconnected departure from the decades of negativity in my head.
The relief in discharge of despair.
I step out into the influencing sphere, the assets of the earth's realm.
The contrasting reality that there is cruelty and hardships in humanity.

I need the connection of my chosen tribe more than ever before,
The gentle prompts in challenges in community habitation.
When fear wavers in, my tribe reminding me of my

journeys so far,
The joining construct in linking with my protecting tribes'.
The shielding support given to me, aiding me in life struggles.

My metaphorical language of my writer's voice,
no longer slumped in the corner of my mind,
no longer in darkness, able to brave the weathers of living.

The strength to give a warm grasp to my heart, in coldness of loss.
My imagination does not harm me; Imagery opens the mind...
Creatively inspiring me whilst trying to make sense of a complexed world...
This an impossible task...
I have many questions of the world and its woes?
I am my own masterpiece, curious in the blemishing blush in my life.

The changing gallery, the visual image, transcribed words from within.

I set up home at the end of 'freedoms journey'.
I validate the courage it has taken to climb over the hills, this part of me needing headspace. I enjoy my new ventures in the townships, smiling regularly in gratitude.
I make new memories with my fellow tribes living alongside me.

There will always be the wonderer in me,
the hippy, carefree part of my escapist expressive soul.

My treasure was not of gold or wealth, the yearning in me was to be accepted, to belong.
To have a voice in depth, in humour in my playful traits.
Living lessons of life, where there is no rule book.
The wish for the fairy-tale ending, I do not wish for the prince or princess.

My fairy tale ending is coming true, I discover stable,

formulation in identity.

The depth in communication,
'A voice'.
'My voice'.
'A journey'.
My part in this universe, the tiny speckle I am in sheer cosmic vastness.

I mastered escapism in childhood, where I stepped into visualisations,
The labyrinth of fantasy…
skipping through the meadows of daisies,
sliding down rainbows,
Jumping on the clouds, landing on the next, like rolling around in fluffy cotton wool.

The adult fantasy giggling, sitting on a cloud with a loved one departed too soon.
Laughing so hard, discussion of time zones, the loved one has not aged.
They are taking me by the hand, in flight through galaxies where the stars never end…

My doable distance, my chosen enhancement, I honour my rights.
The mythopoetically wonder, I take space a room with a view.
Writing as an observer, the witness to my life.
The daily movie like script in my journey, my discovery.
'The temple to my creative escapist soul.'
A personality holding gentleness,
resilience in communication,

release in sharing!

I have taken the scenic route, the blank slate in front of me.
I continue to learn the lessons of village communities, the escapades of the folk of town,
The rapid, swiftness in hustle of the city.

I allow, not panicking in the rush of my inner swirl.
I feel grounded as I regulate the whirl of engagement.
I rest, and reflect on a favourite bench by the sea,
In the times I need to focus and allow stillness.

From the noise in my soul,
in singularity, in community connection with invigorated chatter…
The voice of mine with so much to say…

I am the watchful bystander, my own wise goddess.
I apply focus, fixing, in grounding control in responsibility.

The consistent, reassured greeting from the tribes I have found, ever expanding.
Welcomed, connected, reliable loyalty in trust.
Embodied souls, in bonding,
The furnishing of memories of members of my tribe, some stay with me, some go…

The next episodes in my lifespan,
new beginnings.
Where will they lead to?

The healing I find in communication.
The voice, my voice in society.

My voice
A creative connector.
My voice
'A writer'…

*Illustration by Dawn Skelton*

# Window Ghost

## Emily Polis

### Part One: Something is There

The alcove by the window is never empty. At least, that's what the owners of the house report: 'I could have the heater blasting, it could be a blistering summer's day. No matter what, that alcove by the window is freezing cold. I just never sit over there,' one of the homeowners says. 'There has to be something there. Something that we can't see.'

### Part Two: The Alcove by the Window

It's pleasant today in my little alcove by the window. No one seems to bother me here, I can sit and watch all the people walk by. I wish I could say that the glistening rays of the sun feel good on my skin, or that the ice cream I see people enjoying when they walk by makes me feel a pang of hunger. But sadly, I'm not affected anymore. I've been dead for a little while now, so it's almost hard to remember those seemingly human sensations. Love, desperation, fear, sadness, frustration – unfortunately, I still experience the sensations that those feelings bring. They might manifest through a light tap on a shoulder, the slam of a door, a thump or two on the ceiling. The people in the house have to deal with my emotions alongside me… sorry mom and dad.

# A Soulful Reflection

## Eve Wheeler

I don't think there's any way to get round the fact that I have, and most likely always will be, a rather emotionally sensitive human being. A few weeks ago, I dug out some old school reports and a continuous theme when it came to comments from my general presence in an education setting, was the fact that in many instances, descriptions would fall along the lines of:

'She is a sensitive and observant individual, who often feels overwhelmed in regards to struggling to ask for help if she is struggling with a question or task/assignment during a lesson.'

My school days may be in the past now, a distant memory. But in regards to the general gist of those comments from my school reports, it appears that not much has changed. When I look in the mirror, I still see the same girl. These days my sensitivity may typically, more often than not, be concealed practically entirely under a mask of apparent stoicism. Calmness. Serenity.

I am sure many of us can relate in those complicated and frequently actually quite painful, emotions of vulnerability which most frequently tend to arise when we have one of those days where we wake up and an entire shower of raindrops bounces onto our face as we open our eyes to face the world. Again, the concept of writing this next paragraph fills me with quite significant anxiety. It feels like an emotional replica of that unmistakable feeling of exposure when you arrive at an event and everyone else is already seated in the room. As you navigate your way to your chair, simultaneously you feel around a thousand eyes staring at you, perhaps glazed with confusion or possibly even judgement.

When you are a highly emotional/sensitive person, yet you believe that you must not share your emotions with the world, it feels sort of like you are trying to navigate your way out of a dark forest, without anyone else there to help you guide the way. Intimidating, daunting and downright scary. I can recall many instances in which I have ran to a private location to burst into tears, and then five minutes later I have returned to my seemingly usually calm and stoical self. The storm has passed and the ocean has gone from being plastered with high intensity tsunami force waves, to returning to soft delicate little curls of water, gentle and soothing.

I hope that we can both one day learn to accept the fragility, vulnerability, pain and hope, which accompanies human nature as we weave our way through life.

# A walk in the woodland

## Holly

A walk in the woodland
on a spring day
A carpet of bluebells
under protection of trees
Deer hold their breath
sensing my footsteps
startled they flee
Hares boxing
shielding punches
strongest man wins
Beetles scurry dodging
stomping boots
Hawks gliding
sightseeing for dinner
free-range buffet
The walker stops
hot coffee
sat on a log
watching clouds
meandering
heavy in the sky
The world is silent
Capture glimpse of memories
with a quick photograph

# No Going Back

## Graham Whitton

'That'll be one pound, sir.'

'Three thirty-seven, madam.'

'That'll be two-fifty, young man.'

My name is Ed and this is my life. Or to put more accurately, my hell. Stuck in the same dead end job day in and day out. Having to drag myself out of the depths of depression every morning just to get out of bed at the late, late time of 5am. I'd never even seen a clock at five o'clock until I started this job. I work, to put it bluntly, in a shitty corner shop on a shitty street, selling everything from cheap shitty alcohol to cheap shitty sweets that have fuck all flavour. Seriously you'd get more flavour chewing on a shoelace than any of those sweets we sell. I keep thinking back. Back to the time me and Pete were friends at school... We aren't exactly friends anymore since he took the role of manager. I should mention he also slept with my girlfriend as well and you think that would be the biggest catalyst as to why we aren't besties anymore. But I've wanted out of that relationship for a long time now and Pete gave me the perfect excuse to break it off. I suppose it's the nicest thing he could have done for me these last seven years I've been working at this hell hole.

Anyway, at school in year nine me and Pete had this idea to go into business together. And at the time I had a picture in my head of something like out of Willy Wonka's chocolate factory. Who could've known that all the future held for that business was boredom and misery.

'You're late, Pete,' I said.

'The boss can never be late!' exclaimed Pete. 'He can show up whenever he chooses.'

'Yeah, well when I've got to be here by six in the morning to open and you show up at ten I can't help but feel a little agitated.' I was clearly not happy with his response.

'Careful now Ed, I am the one who pays your bills and I could always find a replacement,' he replied sharply.

'You barely pay me anything,' I moaned. 'It's literally on the dot of minimum wage at seven fifty an hour. Not even a skint university student would work here for that amount of peanuts. And in terms of employment if you do ever get the itch to fire me don't hesitate.'

'Don't tempt me. Now have you made sure all the shelves are stocked?'

'Yes, I did that three hours ago. In fact I've done it about fifty times just to kill time,' I replied sarcastically.

'The job's what you make it Ed, a negative attitude harbours a negative experience.'

'I still think we should have gone with my idea back in school with the arcade,' I said.

But Pete clearly didn't agree. 'Oh really? Arcades aren't even a thing anymore Ed. Not in the UK anyway and from what I've heard they're barely surviving in the US either. The pandemic killed half of them off. But perhaps if you're so keen about it you should try and take your chances in America.'

'Oh yeah,' I replied. 'I'll just catch a plane with the whole fifty quid I have to my name. Maybe I could stand on the runway and hitch one.'

'Enough chitchat Ed, I've got some phone calls to make in the backroom.'

'Yeah, won't be playing slot roulette or anything. Just hard work for you Pete,' I muttered.

He heard that. 'Hey, I'm the one who got the A levels in maths while you got a low C. So that makes me the more qualified one for handling the business,' he boasted. Pete then took out his phone and looked at it as he slowly walked towards the back room.

'You're a c....' Ed muttered under his breath. 'I heard that!' shouted Pete.

Ed let out a big sigh. Why did he do this to himself every day?

Maybe I'd be better taking my chances finding a new job. Or maybe I should just tie a noose round my neck, jump from a stool and be done with it altogether. Nah, too much effort...or maybe I'd suddenly had a devious idea. The shop I worked in was so shit it didn't have any security cameras or alarms on the doors. Pete wanted to save as much money as he could and thought adding any sort of security system would be a big waste of money. Pete liked to think of himself as a bit of a Batman slash super cop type of person. 'I've got eyes and ears everywhere,' he would always say. 'If any thug - or worse, chav - tried to steal from me they would feel the wrath of my fists.' Pete was obsessed with street fighter the video game and ever since he got hooked on it he thought he was Mr Myage. Truth is that although Pete did indeed get an A in maths, he got Es and Fs in pretty much everything else. He took the maths as the most important subject a little too literally from our teacher and flunked every other subject out of pure laziness. I didn't hesitate while Pete was in the backroom. Like a flash he opened the register and took two twenty pound notes and stuffed them in his pockets before closing the register as quick as he opened it. This could work, I thought to himself. Pete suddenly came out the backroom.

'Great news, Ed, I just got a great deal on the new prime hydration drink. Money's about to sky rocket. Damn, you look just about as happy as me about that news.'

'Yes,' I with a grin that would make the grinch blush. 'I'm very happy.'

For next few days I would sample cash from the register, taking enough to make some decent extra money but not enough that dumb-witted Pete would notice. Then those days turned into weeks and then months. A fiver, a tenner, twenty pounds, it all went into my pockets. By the time the next year rolled around I had a new apartment with a swimming pool and a whole bunch of lavish items. As time had gone on I got so confident that I would take notes worth a hundred out of the register, and now I could even afford Sky TV with his new-found fortune. It seemed like the good times would never end. But, as the saying goes, sometimes good things must come to an end.

It was Monday morning and I was whistling and singing different Abba songs to myself. I felt like a new person from the one he was last year. For one, his pockets were a lot heavier. I looked at his watch. Soon customers would start coming into the store putting money into the register where I would then make a sneaky transaction. But little did I know that on this day my days of thievery would hit a bit of a snag. A big bearded man entered the shop. He had a clean-shaven head and tattoos on both his neck and hands.

He spoke in a deep raspy voice, 'I'm the new manager of this store.'

'What?' I said in an almost whimpery tone.

'I said, I'm the new manager of this store, which means I'm also your new boss.'

I was puzzled. 'But what happened to Pete?' I asked in a shaky voice.

'Some kids jumped him wanting to get his wallet. In retaliation he tried to use some sort of karate technique but ended up getting his head smashed in,' Beardy said. 'He won't be back for a long time, if at all. He's in a critical condition at the hospital. Anyway, I'm an old friend of his and two years ago he confided to me in the pub that if anything was to happen to him then he wants me to take over, so here I am.'

My happy morning had quickly turned sour.

'And the first thing I'm going to do as manager,' Beardy said, 'Is to install some much-needed security. Kids out there who jumped him are the kind that will steal anything they can get their fucking, dishonest hands on. Hell, at the moment, you yourself could be stealing from the register and with no security no-one would be any the wiser.'

Beardy laughed. I, unsurprisingly, did not. 'Right, I best get to it then.' Beardy said. 'It's a good job I got an A star in security installation at Brown Bear College.'

Beardy took as little as two hours to set up those cameras. Not only that, but he also installed a security device at the exit so anyone carrying away any unpaid goods would be found out quick.

I sighed. It was over for me. There's no way with this level of security that he could steal from the till anymore. Instead I had to accept that I'm going to be getting such a low income that I wouldn't be able to buy a carboard box for the rest of his life...or...maybe I could try something different.

Gloves, balaclava and prop gun ordered off Amazon, I'm ready to hit it big. With this get up I can walk into that store without being recognised and rob the place. I thought about just accepting my fate as another cog in the machine but the idea of armed robbery is much more exciting and appealing. I put all his robber items of clothing in a Tesco's bag and head down to the corner shop. There's an alleyway about ten feet from the shop, so I slip in there to change. Once in my outfit I put my normal day clothes into his Tesco bag leaving it in the alleyway and, suited up, I walk with haste to the corner shop.

I make sure to make an entrance. I kick open the corner shop door with the prop gun in hand. 'Everyone get on the ground now and no one....' But my demands are cut short.

It's me who gets on the ground, with a giant hole in my

chest.

It turns out that I wasn't the only unsavoury character that worked at this corner shop. You see, Beardy had a bit of a history and he used to work for the local Mafia installing security for them and being a lookout. Not only that, but because he worked in such a dangerous profession, he had learned how to shoot a gun, and the particular gun he became most fond of was a sawn-off shotgun. And it was this shotgun that Beardy used to shoot me.

'Fu... fuck...' I say in a whispery voice. My knees curled up to his chest and my hands clasp to my knees.

Beardy walked over, sawn-off shotgun still in hand. He stood over me and stared me down. 'Well, well, we got ourselves a fucking rat, don't we?'

I put his head to the floor. I could feel myself slowly losing consciousness.

'No-one ever steals from me and gets to live,' said Beardy.

I let out a groan before the world goes black.

'That's going to be one pound, sir.'

'Two-fifteen, young man.'

'Three pounds, mate.'

My name is Tony and I loathe my job. I barely get paid and am severely bored and depressed here. Perhaps it's time I made a career shift. Obviously I can't steal from the register – there's security stuff everywhere. But perhaps to earn some good cash for once I could disguise myself and rob the place....

# Secrets of the Soul

## Hazel Cornhill

The eye sees into your soul
to the darkness within.
You cannot hide from the eye
it pulls out every sin.

The eye sees past the mask
views who you really are.
It matters not if you run
for the eye can view far.

The eye sees your true desires
boring into your soul.
Acceptance is the only way
escape, a futile goal.

# Chaos/Relief

## Julie Daniels

My Great Grandad died of a heart attack when he was hand feeding his horses, cutting the grass with his pocket penknife. He died doing what he loved. He lost his left leg when he was only seven years old and has ever since walked with a crutch. He was of the generation when they mostly rolled their own cigarettes and would love to sit under the dark skies admiring all. He taught me how to roll cigarettes and then light them, whilst having a cuddle, sitting on his one knee. Always happy to do so. Maybe that's why I still smoke after 41 years.

I remember the smells of love surrounding my Great Grandparents' place. They lived in a small caravan parked behind my Great Aunt Janet's place. He loved his horses and to smoke. She loved hard boiled sweets from a hard tinned box for long journeys, or a glass of brandy with some dark chocolates when her tummy was upset.

Ever since he died I couldn't sleep., I had to keep all my cupboards and wardrobe doors closed in my bedroom. I could no longer bear the darkness or of what it would reveal to me. Light was constantly required at night, whether it being a street or a landing light. At one point having had too many sleepless nights I fell asleep at school, actually in class. That was not a good look!

The fear of the darkness has never left me ever since, and I believe it never will. Whilst the darkness can provide chaos it can also provide peace, peace is all I seek. My personal aspirations have always been dictated to by the light. Having looked at everything in my life, my house, my writing, my drawings. Why would my dreams be any different?

Life is a stage show for the non believers. Though I walk down the paths of non fiction I try to breathe. Its shallows encompass the ground to a different sphere. The one you have to adhere to, believe what we read and to provide pictures in our minds.

How can I isolate others' minds, mine and emotions of our hearts and head?

As I sat and listened to the music of life watching also the degrees of many focal points changing in front of my eyes, all my revelations were looking towards the skies. I still am waiting for an answer.

The Moon and the Sun determines our destiny. We are all astronomically inclined by both forces working together.

I walked alone at night to find the sunrise, even though I was scared of the dark. I would walk early in the morning knowing no one was going to be around. I could actually breathe for a moment. No one to judge me. As pure as your first breath as a new born baby.

I would walk with no light pollution in sight apart from my small torch, no one could see me in the dark. I was trying to find some peace, I would totter in my high heel sling back shoes in full makeup and all, with a drink and a cigarette in my hand. My heart was and has always been bleeding with too many emotions every second of the day. Too much to cope with.

For once I could experience some inner peace. No one to judge, all were asleep. Judgement by others has been a continual negative. I would try to glide underneath everyone's radar, none would know that I even exist. I would pray to God and the Fairies at the Bottom of the Garden for it all to stop.

The colossal dark skies with so many lighted spots to shape one's world left me with an understanding of where I stood within the human race, perhaps with a sphere of the lifetime of an Ecologists' hours, all in one go. The darkness of the skies was the right place to start, that was all I could feel. As the light revolves around you the shadows start to lift a little. I stare and wait for that moment, it was one habit that was particularly hard to break. As the Sun escapes from the life of darkness, so do I. I tried to spread the light to enhance and envelope within and around my body. My arms outstretched to feel less pain, unfortunately the wind needed to be blowing in the right direction to assist with my inceptions.

As a sufferer of insomnia I would usually walk at night, what else is there to do? The screaming bah-dabs could always be a choice (if you lived in the middle of no where and had no neighbours). To be able to scream so loud that all my negative emotions would be expelled, from my heart and soul from so far back in my existence I would then breathe, even if I have no voice left.

On rare occasions some sleep was possible, but with so many dark dreams. I would wake up screaming, how much can one take with the constant emotional turmoil my soul receives? How can I silently scream, so that no one can hear?

The walk was almost ceremonial, guessing about 3 km or more. During the years I must have walked that route so many times. No one had a clue, not even my husband who was often left slumbering away in our bed.

I loved the open skies, the smells and the freedom to inhale: that normally wouldn't be allowed. To actually be able to elevate my being to escape from him. As I clipped, clopped down those dark empty Welsh rural lanes I knew by instinct where I needed to aim for. By the sound of my shoes against the different surfaces, the route had become so familiar, I could have walked it with my eyes closed.

Once I had reached that place of peace I would wait for the sunrise for some relief. To breathe. As I watched each time in wonderment of how it would project itself, from the limbs of the Sun to enlighten my life. The body and mind pain becomes one's inconsistencies that are so overwhelming. I needed relief. The sunrise was all I had.

The bird songs afterwards was an incredible feast, enlightened by their music of a full orchestra indeed. Walking home being serenaded by the morning chorus with trumpets of vibrant colours, speared by the limbs of the Octopus. Lights transformed the skies from the dark ink blue galaxies into a swirl of colour.

The Sun has now risen, it is time for me to creep back to bed. No one would ever know.

Every new day is completely untouched, my Mother would always say.

As the Octopus spirits its light and dark colours so do my emotions follow. The uncertainties of life engulfs my being. I become a shallow hal. Less tears, less screams. Its life's limbs slithers out from the dark sea of the sky, the Sun being its torso streaming the rays of cloud or light. The black ink only spews out when it's threatened, resulting in forms of storms of wind, raging hot or momentous floods. I would find peace in watching the explosiveness of all the colours. Clouds parading in front of my eyes. Shadows of depth, light overwhelms. The tentacles of clouds are there to encompass my life's trials, colours of how I could endeavour. Into the arms of comfort.

*Illustrations by Julie Daniels*

# Lunar phases

## Holly

Appear when the world is dreaming
Cycling through moons
sometimes barely visible by night
sometimes awake in daylight
Vanishing
in the opening notes
of dawn

# Do You Remember Oranges?

## Meg Padgett

*[For my Great Aunt, Sybil, who always judged me with so much care.]*

Do you remember oranges?

Each cake at Christmas, carefully crafted with a sprinkling of orange.

A step through the door, to be met with the familiar scent of your carefully crafted Christmas cake.

Do you remember oranges?
Do you remember Capri-suns?

Your fridge, forever flowing with an over-abundance of capri-suns, waiting.

Waiting for us.

Do you remember oranges?
Do you remember Capri-suns?
Do you remember glitter?

Your face, turned to complete confusion upon seeing my tiny pot of sparkling silver.

Moments later, your face turned into one of admiration of that same tiny pot of sparkling silver.

Do you remember oranges?
Do you remember Capri-Suns?
Do you remember glitter?
Do you remember?

If I showed you an orange now, would you remember it, or would your memory continue to muddle?

The oranges, lost.

# The life of John Ronald Reuel Tolkien

## Mary C Palmer

### Introduction

I dreaded the last of my Creative Writing assignments which was *'The Hobbit'* by John Ronald Reuel Tolkien. I dreaded getting to this final assignment because it was not my reading or writing genre but I had no choice and so, I began…

### The Unexpected Party

I knew my concentration levels were going to be challenged, so I decided to make notes in the margin as I read through the script.

### Part One: The first chapter of The Hobbit

Tolkien began to describe the hole in the ground where The Hobbit lived:

*Not a nasty, dirty, wet hole, not filled with ends of worms and an oozy smell, nor yet a dry, bare, sandy hole with nothing in it to sit down on or to eat it was a Hobbit hole.*

I immediately got the impression of shored up trenches, dug out during wartime. The Hobbit's home was built in a hole in the ground.

He described the many bathrooms and bedrooms; lots of cellars and pantries. Whole rooms that were devoted to clothes alone. Kitchens, dining rooms, all on the same floor and indeed along the very same passage. The best rooms were all on the left-hand-side (going in) for these were the only ones to have windows, deep-set round windows looking over his garden and meadows beyond, sloping down to the river. All with very fine decor and luxurious furnishings. It was then that I knew he had, at some time in his life, experienced living in these types of surroundings and that he had come from a well to do family; from a family that had enjoyed the wealth and comfort of such luxurious surroundings.

## Part Two: Curiosity got the better of me

By now, I was so curious to find out where JRR Tolkien was drawing his fantasy writing from and I felt compelled to explore; to find out more and that was where I became hooked. I wanted to know: 'what had this man experienced in his life to form this style of writing?' And I couldn't leave it there.

## Part Three: Where his life began

Tolkein was born on the 3rd January 1892 in Bloemfontein (*The City of Roses)* the largest free state in South Africa, known as the judicial capital. The first languages being: Afrikaans, Sotho, English, Xhosa & Tswana.

## His parents: Arthur and Mabel

Arthur Reuel Tolkien (1857-1896) was an English Bank Manager. His wife Mabel had left England when Arthur was promoted to head of the Bloemfontein office of the British Bank for which he worked. He had descended from a long line of middle-class high-quality craftsmen who made and sold clocks, watches and pianos in Birmingham.

The Tolkien family originated in the East Prussian town

of Kreuzburg near Konigsburg which had been founded during the mediaeval German Eastward expansion. Tolkien's family emigrated to London in the 1770's and became the ancestors of the English family. His second Great-Grandfather in 1792; Benjamin Tolkien and William Gravell took over the Erdely Norton factory and from then on sold clocks and watches under the name of Gravell and Tolkien. Most of his family had evacuated from East Prussia.

## Part Four: Visit to England

Tolkien's mother took 3-year-old John and his younger brother to Birmingham, England on what was intended to be a lengthy family visit. His father, however, developed rheumatic fever and died in, South Africa before he could join them, and this left the family without an income. Mabel Tolkien was received into the Roman Catholic Church in 1900 despite vehement protests by her Baptist family, which stopped all financial assistance to her.

Tolkien's mother then took him to live with her parents in Kings Heath, Birmingham - which amazingly happens to be where I lived in Birmingham. He went to the same Catholic school as my cousin Dorothy and attended a school at the end of the road where I later lived. His mother educated him well and he was an excellent pupil, always eager to learn anything & everything she taught him, which happened to be a lot about botany and awakened in him his joy in the look and feel of plants. His favourite lessons were languages and his mother taught him the fine rudiments of Latin. He liked reading about the Native American Red Indians & disliked The Pied Piper, Treasure Island and Alice in Wonderland and, the latter he found very disturbing; which was actually written by his dear friend, Lewis Carroll.

## Part Five: Aged 12; John's mother dies

When John was 12 years old his mother very sadly died of acute diabetes at the very young age 34. Insulin would not be discovered until two decades later in 1921.

Mabel died at Fern Cottage in Rednal, Birmingham which she had been renting.

After her death Tolkien wrote *"it is not to everybody that God grants so easy a way to his great gifts as he did to my brother and I, giving us a mother who killed herself with labour and trouble to ensure us keeping the faith."* (Carpenter: 1977)

## Part Six: Father Xavier Morgan

Before her death Tolkien's mother Mabel had assigned the guardianship of her sons to her close friend, Father Xavier Morgan of the Birmingham Oratory to bring them up as good Catholics.

In a later letter to his son Michael, Tolkien, recalled the influence of the man he called, Father Francis, how he first learned charity and forgiveness from him and, in the light of it pierced even the darkest times in his life.

## Part Seven: Education

Tolkein grew up in Edgbaston, Birmingham and went to King Edward's school where he won a foundation scholarship. In his early teens John and his two cousins, Mary & Marjorie invented a new and complex language called, Nevbosh but he also went on to invent many more languages.

## Part Eight: Edith Mary Bratt

As a teenager at the tender age 16, Tolkien met Edith Mary Bratt, 3 years his senior. They took to frequenting the tea shops in Birmingham, where friendship blossomed into love & romance. Both were orphans, in need of love and affection and that, they could give to each other and by now they were in love. However, his guardian, Father Morgan considered it altogether unfortunate that his surrogate son was romantically involved with an older, Protestant woman and Father Morgan prohibited Tolkien from; meeting, talking or corresponding with Edith until he was 21 & if he didn't obey, he would cut short his university.

## Part Nine: A proposal of undying love

On the evening of his 21st birthday Tolkien wrote to Edith & declared his undying love for her and, a proposal of marriage. However, Edith had agreed to marry another, only because she thought Tolkien no longer cared for her. On the 8th of January 1913 Tolkien travelled to meet Edith and as they sat talking and listening to each other under the railway viaduct, she agreed to marry him. Edith wrote to end the engagement of her former proposal and returned the engagement ring. The family were deeply insulted and angry saying that Tolkien was a cultured gentleman with no prospects and extremely poor.

Following their engagement Edith reluctantly announced that she was converting to Catholicism, at Tolkien's insistence. Edith Bratt and Ronald Tolkien were married at St Mary Immaculate Catholic Church on March 22nd 1916. In a later letter to his son in 1941 he expressed his "*admiration, for his wife's willingness to marry a man with no prospects and little money except, the likelihood of being killed in the Great War.*" (Carpenter and Tokein, 1981)

## Part Ten: Posted to France

On the evening before being posted to France the Tolkiens spent their night in a room at the Plough and Harrow hotel in Edgbaston, Birmingham. He wrote: *Junior officers were being killed off a dozen a minute* and of parting from his wife: *it was like death. (Garth, 2003).* During the crossing to Calais he wrote a poem 'The Lonely Isle', inspired by his feelings during the crossing (Garth, 2003):

**The Lonely Isle by RR Tolkien**

For me for ever they forbidden
marge appears
A gleam of white rock over
sundering seas,
And thou art crowned in glory
through a mist of tears,
Thy shores all full of music, and thy
Lands of ease - Old haunts of many children robed in flowers,
Until the sun pace down his arch of hours,
When in the silence fairies with a
wistful heart Dance to soft airs their harps and.
viols weave.

## Part Eleven: Writing in Code

To evade the British Army censorship he wrote to Edith in code, so she could track his every movement on a map of the western front. He'd written how he and his men were being eaten by hordes of lice & the ointment they used made the lice even more ravenous.

He caught Trench fever (a disease carried by lice) and was invalided to England on the 8th November 1916.

## Part Twelve: War Time

In later years Tolkien spoke to his daughter about being at the front, the horrors of the first German gas attack, the utter exhaustion; the whirling scream of shells and endless marching on foot through a devastated landscape, sometimes, carrying men's equipment as well as his own to encourage them to keep going. Some remarkable relics had survived from that time: a trench map he drew himself and pencil written orders to carry bombs to the fighting line.

Many of his dearest friends were killed; sadly, Rob Gilson was killed on the first day at the Somme. A weak and emaciated Tolkien alternated between hospitals and garrison duties, medically deemed unfit for general service.

He began recovering in a cottage in little Haywood, Staffordshire where he began to work on what he called, *'The Book of Lost Tales'* beginning with, *The Fall of Gondolin*; representing his first attempt at mythology.

## Part Thirteen: Edith Dies

In 1916 his first son was born and he was promoted to lieutenant where he was stationed at Kingston upon Hull.

## Part Fourteen: After the War

After the war he worked at the Oxford Dictionary, on the history of etymology of words of Germanic origin beginning with the letter W. He then took up a post as Reader in English language at University of Leeds. While at Leeds he produced A Middle English Vocabulary.

He began to tutor undergraduates and following his

time at Pembroke college Tolkien wrote *The Hobbit* and the first two volumes of *Lord of the Rings*.

## Part Fifteen: World War II

In the run up to the Second World War Tolkien was earmarked in the war office as a code breaker. In 1939, he was asked to serve in the Codebreaker department of the Foreign Office. In 1945 he moved to Merton College, Oxford, becoming Professor of English Language and Literature, taking his retirement in 1959. He served as an External Examiner for University College in Galway and received an honorary degree from the National University of Ireland.

He completed *Lord of the Rings* in 1948, a decade after his first sketches.

## Part Sixteen: The Later Years

Tolkien had four children and he was very devoted to them, sending them illustrated letters from Father Christmas.

From retirement in 1959 up to his death 2nd September 1973 he continued to receive public attention and literary fame. Even C. S. Lewis nominated him for the Nobel prize in literature.

Fan attention became so intense that he had to take his phone number out of the public directory.

Tolkien and Edith had moved to Bournemouth, a seaside beautiful resort patronised by the British upper middle class and Tolkien's status as a bestselling author gave them easy entry into polite society but Tolkien deeply missed his fellow Inklings. Edith, however, was overjoyed to step into the role of a society hostess, which is why

Tolkien chose Bournemouth in the first place.

He gave up his life at Oxford so she could retire to Bournemouth and in her pride of him becoming a famous author. They were tied together by the love of their children and grandchildren. Edith died on the 29th November 1971 aged 82.

After his wife's death Tolkien remembered: "I never called Edith Luthien - but she was the source of the story that in time became the chief part of the *Silmarillion*." (Carpenter and Tolkein, 1981) It was first conceived in a small woodland glade, filled with Hemlocks at Roos in Yorkshire: "where I was in command, of an outpost of the Humber Garrison in 1917 and she was able to live with me for a while). In those days her hair was raven, her skin clear, her eyes brighter than you have seen them and she could sing - and dance. But the story has gone crooked and I am left and I cannot plead before the inexorable Mandos." (ibid.)

After her death Tolkien returned to Oxford, where Merton College gave him convenient rooms near the High Street. He missed Edith but enjoyed being back in the City.

## Part Seventeen: Order of the British Empire

Tolkein was made a Commander of the order of the British Empire in 1972 and received the insignia of the order at Buckingham Palace by Her Majesty Queen Elizabeth II.

He had the name Luthien engraved on Edith's tombstone and when Tolkien died 21 months later on the 2nd of September 1973 aged 81, he was buried in the same grave with Beren added to his name.

Tolkien's will was proven on 20th December 1973 with his estate valued at £190,577 equivalent to £2,452,000 in 2021.

I hope that in reading this essay, as I have in writing it, you have reached some conclusions about the life experiences portrayed in his writing.

## References

Carpenter, H. (1977). *Tolkien: A Biography*. New York: Ballantine Books

Carpenter, H. and Tolkien, C, eds. (1981). *The Letters of J. R. R. Tolkien*. London: George Allen & Unwin.

Garth, John (2003). *Tolkien and the Great War*. Harper-Collins

# The Sky has Many Faces

## Tamar Driscoll

The sky has many faces,
What will it be today?
Sometimes it can be blissful, beautiful and warm,
Sometimes it's cold, horrid, wet and it makes you hide away,
What is your preference, do you feel you get a say?

I feel people are like the weather,
We all feel many skies throughout the day.
We experience changes that are good, but also sad moments that fill us with dismay.
This can sometimes weather are moods and I'm not to proud to say,
I definitely have damp, dull, dark days.

And this is when I don't like myself,
And I will tell you why.
Its because I am dealing with the storm, The storm I hold inside.
I want to be what everyone expects,
But like the weather I can't always control
I want to be the rainbow that they want to love, cherish and hold.

But when my storm comes,
I feel I make a real mess,
Even though it only say a quick hello,
I feel it courses distress.

But sometimes I don't like myself,
I hope it's not contagious.
I try every day to make better discussions, think more, count to ten, make changes.

But like the weather in the world,
we can predict but we can't control.
The happiness it can sometimes bring but also the sorrow and destruction it also can behold.

I do have a lot of sunny days to,
That fills me and others with joy.
I feel this is when I'm at my best,
I feel real happiness and joy.

The sky has many faces
And I have a few too.
We except the weather's no matter what it is,
And maybe one day I can accept myself too.

# Natural Peel

## Milly Watson

'And in the depths of the well,
Where it dwells - *it* dwells -
Skin peels back to reveal something beneath,
Something born of hate,
Of loathing,
Of absolute despair and debasement,
A festering, stinking pustule of misery.
It seeps inside,
It finds you, every bit of yourself you want gone, that you can't bare to look at in the mirror, that causes you to feel an urge to vomit and it twists,
It coils and warps and makes the bone rise up from beneath,
The veins pop out and all you can see is the raw redness beneath, hidden by your flesh, the very thing it has to savage to get you to see,
Make you see,
What's beneath,
What you want gone,
What causes you so much unrest,
What you hate'

Dear Trez,

As requested, please find the poem sample enclosed. I'll admit to you, my German's gotten pretty rusty since the good old GCSE days, and I had to bite back the urge to make grammatical edits.

Accuracy aside, it feels unfair. The least I can do is give these people the decency of echoing their final words properly, instead of twisting things just for my own preferences. The curse of the linguist, I suppose you'd say.

I haven't seen much of the outside since touching down, and honestly, I don't want to.

It's the worst phrasing I have, but my skin feels too tight already.

Exploration could get me in contact with whatever the hell that stuff is, and for all Asheter insists we've got nothing to worry about - safety precautions, state of the art hazmat suits, saliva tests, blood tests, hair follicle tests, the most accurate microbe testing yada yada blah blah - I can't join in his enthusiasm for poking and prodding every rock we see.

If I'd gotten a proper say, I wouldn't have even gone past the village signpost, but that choice wasn't in my hands.

At first I kept telling myself it was some grotesque avant garde art installation. That we'd been duped into serving as the first visitors to some boundary breaking project (probably some 'visionary' ordering about their army of gophers), in some ingenious publicity stunt where the egg on our faces would lure in critics and connoisseurs of the real mind-bending stuff.

But really that was just to keep myself from hysteria.

The first real thing I wanted was to be sick.

Jesus Trez, if you'd seen the insides of that house, the first little one in a government mandated row of two-up, two-downs, so unassuming and innocuous it made you feel safe. Then you stepped over the threshold and came face-to-face with Hell.

It was as if they'd been torn apart. Insides first.

Their bodies were twisted beyond what even the worst nightmares could offer. New limbs sprouting from backs and forearms, the stubby edges of premature fingernails climbing up throats, extra eyes dotting foreheads and maws gaping on kneecaps. They hadn't even gotten a chance to move from where the transformation began.

Sprawled like ragdolls across sofas, slumped on kitchen chairs, limp in bathtubs...

There was so much blood in that place, staining the walls, the furniture, what remained of the people; it became hard to tell where clothing ended and skin began. Some of the appendages had ripped cleanly through denim, linen and cotton, while others hadn't quite managed to break the barrier, too weak when they surged.

Kat can't quite tell if the infection comes in varying stages, perhaps depending on your initial point of contact. She's been holed up in the lab since Day 3 and I doubt we'll be seeing much more of her, at least for the next five days, as she prods samples, comparing and contrasting enzymes, all the nitty gritty stuff I've never been good at.

Everywhere I looked fresh clumps could be found. Matted hair and scraps of bone, broken clean when the adjustments for a new shape took place in spasms and convulsions. Globs caked the wallpaper and plaster in new layers. I didn't dare touch anything, not even with three pairs of gloves on, but Spence was crazy enough to give it a try: said it was spongey, like uncooked meat. Then I really did have to fight the urge to throw up.

I swallowed a bit of bile back, but I don't think anyone realised I'd just puked in my mouth. They wouldn't have let me hear the end of it.

Trez, you have to promise me, when this letter arrives, that what I'm about to say is just going to be kept between the two of us. At least for now.

I didn't mean to eavesdrop, it just happened when I was on my way to the showers. Kat and Hina have never been any good at keeping their voices down...so I just overheard, like I have done a thousand times when they get all Out Sciencing each other. But this was different.

They don't think the cell tissue's entirely dead.

The Landespolizei weren't lying when they swore they

blitzed the majority of the land - just for safe measure - but even a good dose of dry ice can't see everything dead in its tracks.

If that shit's alive, I can't trust Asheters' words. That we're safe from infection. That we're not all going to see ourselves twist into those gargoyles, human Rorschach tests, deforming into something unbearable, something so malformed and grotesque...

Trez you haven't seen it, you couldn't possibly know but I...

If someone got infected, the kindest thing to do would be to kill them.

Hina hasn't been able to confirm when death occurred, before or after the worst of the mutative process had set in. She'd kill me for saying it, but I think part of her's scared to find out.

The thought of being alive - as you start to sprout new arms and legs, see mouths emerge on your stomach, grow antlers from your scalp as the bones unravel and extend - with all that happening to you, too lethargic to move, the blood loss being your only respite from the pain...I'd rather be dead than go through that.

Spence, Faraday and Rawley? They see this as some grand adventure. A great tour into the unknown. Our first promise of glory and status. That we're going to come back with all the answers and spare such a curse from unleashing again.

But I can't shake the feeling their giddiness could doom us all.

If the virus isn't dead, how do we know there's no chance it could resurface? And what might a new incubation period be?

I'm not a scientist, so how could I even answer any of my own questions? I'm just the translator.

The phones are still playing up. Danni's been trying their

best - spending hours hunched over the fuse boxes, fiddling and digging with their kit - but so far, we only have the emergency mobile working, and Asheter's been clear it's absolutely banned from personal use. I guess so we don't fuck up and have that lost too.

His backwards faith continues to be a headache: none for us, but absolute assurance there's nothing to fear in this village.

I pray we won't be infected

Wait for another letter from me Trez. If Danni can't work their magic, I guess that's how you'll know.

Yours faithfully,
*Jenna*

# The Dance of Light and Darkness: A Wanderer's Odyssey

## Jacob Huitt

'No!' a masculine yell echoed through the streets. Beneath the soundwaves of the frightened soul, walked a lone wanderer. With the flicker of flame emitting from a cigarette, the shadow of the distant figure approached.

The sky above was cloudless and birdless. But hovering within the sandbox of nothing, was the moon, blessing the waterlogged streets, densely populated homes, and sleeping trees with its gaze.

The figure walked towards the origin of the yell out of instinct, foolish or brave, the unknown is a cruel thing. With the fog of fear guarding the gates of oblivion, nobody dared enter but him. Ending up in a movie theatre of soul-wrenching melancholy and exfoliated fear of the future, the man found his seat in a large room with walls overgrown in rose flowers.

'Where am I now,' the somewhat unfazed man said to himself with an ironic tone, periodically taking a puff of his cigar. As he sat, content, and in control, the dark room was lit up by the bright lights of the theatre projector, displaying a looping clip of soldiers in uniform at a table, laughing, cheering, all the while audio promoted the idea of men joining the army.

The theatre suddenly grew warmer. Within the same instance, his heart started violently beating, eyes dilated; accidentally gripping his smoke too hard, turning it into mush. With his eyes locked on the bright screen, whilst in the background the clicking of the film grew evidently louder, it was now known that control was absent.

His head enveloped and tightened, suffocating on the past, like a snake around a tree. Fear is a tether to all minds, one of which controls more than you can think. As for the lone man, he braved once, and now he must repeatedly brave furthermore. That be at the sight of what life used to be, or the hearing of sirens, gunshots, and screams, constantly fighting to save all, even those he knowingly cannot save. This urge to save overlooks one major factor, one major character, and that is the urge to save oneself. The reflection he saw in the puddle of the storm was of a man who was destined to be sacrificed for others.

All the while imprisoned by the mind, the theatre doors slammed open. To the lone wanderer's lacking awareness, a man had come to accompany him. The new body made himself known to the other by sitting adjacent.

With a concerned, but rather passive voice the man asked awkwardly, 'Linden? You alright?'

A response was expected, but one was not granted. For Linden was continuing to hyperventilate whilst trapped in a trance of sluggishness, staring into the bright screen, and lost in panic.

The man who came to speak to Linden stood up rapidly upon noticing the state of his friend, rushed up the stairs into the back room, and ripped the film out of the projector, leaving a rancid smell, and echoed bang throughout the theatre, replacing the audio from the tape, leaving the room dimly lit. It was not until he returned that he found Linden holding his face in disappointment and out of breath.

'Are you okay?' the man said to Linden while calmly getting comfortable. Kicking his feet up onto the seat in front, he reached for a pack of smokes and a lighter.

'Yes,' Linden said firmly, pulling himself from his covered face and glaring straight into the man's eyes.

'Woah there bud, calm yourself. You want one?'

Linden first pulled his thick brown hair back with his

wet muddy hands. Then the man tapped his shoulder with a cigar and nodded for him to take it.

'I suppose so... Thanks,' he said whilst gathering his breath, taking a whiff, an exhale, and the cherry on top, a hard yawn.

Linden leaned back in his chair and looked at the man on his right.

'Why are you here, Garrett?'

'Ay, you know me, I can't sit still. I noticed you haven't replied to my mail in ages, thought to myself, maybe I should spare a visit. Quite good timing don't you think?'

As a moment of silence seeped in between responses, the thundering outside shook the building, like a giant making its way through the streets.

'I was fine, Garrett, don't start inflating your ego; I was fine.'

'Bollocks that mate, I saw your face, you were back in the trenches.'

Admitting defeat, Linden took a puff more of his new cigarette and responded, 'Knowing that it is coming back again: the day where I will have to steal from another, like the last yell of my first victim. I don't think there is a way out for me, other than, I suppose, the inevitable.'

'A way out? Come on man, look at yourself. You not only were forced to leave your small town for the first time but to shoot a weapon larger than a pistol and to meet people from the big cities. Then you were pushed into fighting a war you didn't even know began. You crossed the channel with me and fought alongside me. We lost, we gained, we bruised, and were drained. You did what needed to be done. What changed?'

Reminiscing over all the accomplishments he has under his name, Linden's eyes began to glow. Memories of time spent with family, pets, and the misfortune of being caught in the rain. Time spent walking through snickets and woodlands alone. The smiles, the drooping faces of loss, the dark, the bright, the hopeful, and the hopeless: clouded grey overhead. As time may prove death inevitable, so too are periods of joy. This Is the gift of living.

Gazing into the mind's conjurations of life as it played out before him, Linden began to mumble:

I am my own best friend, and my worst enemy, my own blizzard and raging storm.
I am my drowning sorrows, my scars from yesterday; my only hope to reach those tomorrows.

I am my own person, alone I may be, but stand, I can always guarantee.
I am my own motivation, the book, never-ending story; robbed of the possible mindful glory.

I was my own killer, my abuser, my rekindled swinging of the baseball bat.
I was scared, alone I fought; endured like the last standing pillar.

I was my stench, my lacking mercy, and my probable death.

Now, I, Lone wanderer, soon to take his final breath, will fight what is blacking, sat upon my idle backbench. I will watch the bees buzz, the butterflies fly, and the birds dance, whilst deer in the back... still prance...

I will die, but not now. I never got to say a proper

goodbye.

Shifting back into the present, shedding a tear of appreciation onto a bouquet of rose flowers, Linden placed the flowers on Garrett's grave and made his leave.

# A Soundtrack To My Childhood - Pieces of Memoir

## Esther Clare Griffiths

Mondays were a mix of sleepy leavings and queasy dread. Even before the birds began to sing, Mum would stroke my head and waken me gently in whispers. I'd stumble, still warm, half-asleep into a cold car, twisting round to watch Ballygelly fade fast out of the back window. Within a few sharp minutes, our little cottage with white-washed walls and bright red window frames sank away from me, like waves seeping into sand. Huddled on the back seat with my wee brother, Jesse, we watched the quiet dark of rolling hills give way to bright lights and traffic jams. Sure, in one swift hour, we swapped Ballygelly's calm green valleys and meandering pathways for the tense city suburbs of Belfast and school.

Our first rented house, Fitzroy Avenue, was a large, tumbling, old building divided into flats. We had the ground floor and all four of us slept in one sprawling room. After Ballygelly, it seemed airy and spacious. A wide, Victorian staircase led to a luxuriously large bathroom, with a long, metal key. When Anna and Keavy came to play, we would do everything to stop them leaving. Once, Anna and I locked ourselves in the bathroom when it was time to go home. For a while we relished being locked away - large, jellied sweets shaped like an orange and a lemon whiled away the time. We lay in the empty bath fully clothed and laughed and laughed. Our parents eventually asked us to open up, calling 'home time' gently and then more forcefully. I tried to open the door but the key jammed. We pulled and wrestled with the old key, shaking the door, leaning our little frames hard against the wood, but it wouldn't budge. I panicked, first rattling the door, then shouting, 'We can't get out!' Fear rising in my throat, sweeping away all the laughter from the empty bath. 'Stand back!' Dad commanded. Anna and I huddled close, our hands tightly intertwined, our eyes glued to the door. We held our breath to the sound of splintering wood as the entire door caved over. We froze, clinging to each other, the taste of jellied fruit forever mingled with sheer terror. Anna and I ran to our mums who held us tight, rocking us back and forth, back and forth, fear fading, ebbing way, like a boat docked at last.

Soon after this, I came home from school to find my mum waiting in the garden for me - the entire facade of our house lay crumbled like a sandcastle in heaps of dusty rubble. Years of bomb blasts and neglect had taken its toll – all I could think about was the box of After Eight chocolates in the kitchen. We were allowed one crispy emerald packet with its golden clock before bed. I remembered my little shop in our bedroom - a brown till with cream buttons and a cash register that shot open to the sound of a bell. Jesse and I set up a sweetie shop with dolly mixtures, chocolate buttons and wine gums. I would be the shop keeper and he was my faithful customer. We never saw our shop again and strangely we never asked, accepting it had gone, feeling lucky we were alive and had Ballygelly as our real home.

Once Fitzroy Avenue disintegrated into dust, we moved across town to Wellington Park - a flat near the Botanic Gardens. My brother and I loved our bedroom - it had once belonged to an old lady who needed help, and there was a long cord with a wooden bobble hanging above our bunkbeds that rang a bell in the kitchen. We were soon playing servants and hospitals, running back and forth from the tiny, galley kitchen to our room, trays of treats wobbling, almost tipping over. A tropical fish tank lit up our whole bedroom at night, casting a sea glow over all my dreams. Before I drifted off to sleep, I'd stretch my hand from the top bunk to trace the bumpy wallpaper, loving the pink roses that climbed in a delicate sprawl right up to the edges of our ceiling - imagining the old lady pulling her cord and looking at the very same rose filled walls.

One night, I was in my pyjamas watching the tropical fish, Jesse was still in the bath, when there was a knock at the door. I was fascinated to see a policeman standing there in full uniform, hat in hand. He said we needed to leave the building immediately as there had been a bomb scare. I was only dimly aware of what this meant, but I understood it was serious. My brother was hauled dripping from the bath, just wrapped in a towel. I had time to shove on some shoes and pull a duffel coat over my pyjamas. Then we were out in the cold, dark night, bundling into the car, our breath misting the windows in great freezing clouds. We stayed up late with friends I scarcely knew, eating yellow rice and curry in a hubbub of merriment. My brother was offered a lemon as a joke, but to everyone's shock and great amusement, he sucked the lemon dry and asked for more. Adults always seemed to be laughing at things I didn't find especially funny!

That night, I woke early, wondering where I was and why; the clean, starched sheets reeked of washing powder - I knew instantly I wasn't at home! Then I remembered the policeman, and the cold air clouds in the car, and the adults laughing as Jesse drained a lemon. It all washed over me in a cold sweat. I lay quietly wishing I was back in my top bunk with the soothing sound of bubbles spilling up into our tropical fish tank, the iridescent flash of blue and red neon tetras - and my dreams forever immersed in an aqua glow.

Once school was over, we went back to our flat, and the French Embassy building next door with its grand, Grecian stone pillars was a pile of rubble. I didn't understand how it had happened, much less why, but my dad, who was a keen historian and discoverer of life, let us sift around in the damp, charcoaled remnants, searching for anything not completely burnt to cinders. We picked up French journals and magazines, fragments of sooty pages soon disintegrating in our hands. Partially buried, hidden amongst the scorched sandstone, we came across a map, curled and blackened at the edges. With his shirt sleeve, Dad gently smoothed away a layer of soot to reveal a huge map of France in muted pinks, purples, greens and blues. Each area, once a vivid segment of colour, was dusted in a thick coating of black. The map still hangs on our wall, a stark reminder of violence and survival. For me, it was treasure looted from a fire, I could see the charcoaled remnants, the blackened edges, but I didn't really connect it with the bomb scare. My brother and I soon returned to pulling the cord for a servant and stacking trays precariously high, lost in our little worlds, just momentarily aware of a wider, fragmented world outside our window.

Finally, Friday came around – forever imbued with a vast sense of relief and escape. In a heartbeat, I swapped the cloying dread of school and the vivid streets of Belfast, for green valleys and our haven, Ballygelly cottage. My brother and I would jump back into our battered old car, eyes alight as we searched for the twisting, narrow lanes to lead us home again. Hour upon hour of giddy freedom with friends – swinging from rope swings, playing hide and seek in the fields, jumping from haybales, and chatting till late - safe in the darkness of Ballygelly rafters. We even roamed beyond Ballygelly with our pals - pockets laden with cheese, raisins and apples.

Our favourite walk led us up a winding hillside to an old lady's sweetie shop. We would knock on the door of her house and she would lead us across the crumbling yard to her shop - a dilapidated shed crammed full of sweets. She was barely any taller than us, a tiny lady with grey hair scraped into a bun and clickety-clack black boots – just like Mrs Pepperpot. As she measured our wine gums on her old bronze scales, I'd imagine her suddenly shrinking, so we would open our paper bag to find a miniature old lady scrambling amongst a jungle of sticky sweets. Blackcurrant, raspberry, tangerine, lemon and lime – all in diamonds, ovals and perfect spheres. Each shelf was packed full of glass sweetie jars, the stickers faded and curling in clumps around the sides - just a whisper of their former glory. Despite the vast array of choice, we always plumped for wine gums, and I liked swapping yellow and orange for black or red, tracing the letters of each sweet with my fingers before jamming my teeth together with their hard glue chewiness. The words etched into the wine gums in bumpy letters were *claret, port, sherry, burgundy* and other drinks we'd never heard of - they felt foreign, intriguing in their obscurity. Perhaps the little old lady had once had a thriving business but I felt almost sure we were her only customers. Her shed of sweeties lay hidden, deep in the heart of Irish fields, chequered in uneven, emerald patchwork and stretching on towards the sea. A faded sign *'sweet shop'* was glued to the shed window, peeling, tattered at the edges, and so pale it must have been there a very long time. Time had bleached and mottled it with damp - any passing cars would surely miss it. We always stopped and she always unlocked the shed, measuring out a seemingly endless supply of wine gums. Only once, we knocked eagerly on the door and were baffled when there was no reply. We tried several times before turning away bitterly disappointed and with nothing to carry our little legs home.

# Anti-ode to Small Creatures

## Ellie King

O beetle
Whyfor art thou here?
Thine scuttling doth
beget my fear

My only wish
from heart so true
is that an oaf
should tread on you
and crush thine body
to the floor
so thou shouldst be
not nevermore

But you foul slug
are so much worse
Thy very being
is a curse
and I'm afraid
that I'm averse
to you
and all your kind

You ruin days of gardening
Attempts to mow the lawn
must end when you come slithering
I flee inside, forlorn

But hark! Now comes the postman
And is my dream come true?
He bears a pack of Nemaslug
and it's the end for you

# Miss Nicely Returns

## Virginia Sellar-Edmunds

'Is that the one you want?'

The young man behind the counter of the burger joint beheld the rather dithery customer with growing concern. She seemed never to have had a burger before, and he was progressively more anxious about finding the right meal for her. Add to that the fact that he had had a bad experience with an elderly lady, which ended with him having to leave his previous job as an usher at the local theatre and to have to take up serving burgers for a living. As a result of that experience Roddy hated serving old ladies – he found them too unpredictable. Fortunately his workmates were very understanding and generally took over serving the more elderly customers. Today, however, everyone else was already busy, so Roddy had to bite the bullet and serve the dear old dithery lady himself.

The blood was rushing to Roddy's head as he repeated 'Is that the one you want?'

'Well dear,' began Miss Nicely, 'if that's the one that you recommend.'

Roddy was disconcerted by the rush of responsibility. Usually, the customer knew what they wanted and told him so. He started to sweat and had to keep wiping it out of his eyes with his shirt sleeve.

'Right madam, so that will be one special burger with complementary beverage. Which beverage would you prefer?'

'I think I would like a nice cup of tea, if that is possible of course', replied Miss Nicely.

'Certainly madam' Roddy was unfailingly polite to all of

his customers, including this strange old lady.

'I'll just nip into the ladies' room while you get it ready for me.'

'Certainly madam' replied Roddy.

Roddy was starting to have his suspicions about the dithery old lady. She reminded him of someone, and he couldn't quite think who. Then, just as she opened the toilet door, it came to him who she was – the old lady who had been the catalyst of all his troubles. He swallowed valiantly as he started to feel nauseous.

At that moment a strikingly flame haired young woman strode out of the toilet, she was dressed in black leathers and stunning biker boots. She threw a £10 note on the counter in front of Roddy and snapped:

'That's for the meal that the silly old woman was in the process of buying. Keep the change.'

Realising that Miss Nicely had done another disappearing act, Roddy slid to the floor in a dead faint, coming round a few minutes later to find himself in the centre of a circle of worried colleagues, wondering what they should do. After plying Roddy with a glass of water to be sipped slowly they ordered a taxi for him, and the manager told him to take the rest of the day off to recover.

Vixen LeStrange strode down the street muttering to herself about how the idiot Leticia Nicely had nearly defiled 'the body' with a burger and fries. At least she had kept away from cola or milkshakes. About 200 yards down the road, she realised that she had forgotten her 1952 Vincent Black Lightening. It would be wherever Letitia Nicely had left her trusty old sit up and beg, Pegasus. Vixen turned on her heel and marched back to the burger joint. Now, where would be the best place to leave a bike? After looking around for a minute or so, she alighted on the alley at the side of the building – ah yes there was the motorbike just waiting for her.

Unfortunately, as Vixen prepared to depart on her bike her nose began to itch. That was the sign that she was about to turn into Miss Nicely, who was needed somewhere to sort out some sort of trouble. Vixen sighed and took a very small umbrella out of the panniers of her bike. The hedge was too small to perform the transformation in private, so Vixen reluctantly went down the insalubrious alley again. Once she was sure that no one would see her from the road she opened the umbrella and began to twirl it in front of her. After a few twirls Mis Nicely appeared and the umbrella which was now golf size was promptly neatly furled ready to be stashed in Pegasus's basket.

Letitia now exited from the alley in search of Pegasus. She located him lying on his side in front of what she would call the 'café'. She felt as though he was giving her a baleful look and spent no time at all righting him. The golf umbrella was safely stowed in his basket which was much larger inside than out, and always contained just what was needed. Even Miss Nicely wasn't quite sure by what mechanism that worked, but she used it and always thanked Pegasus when she returned an item.

Letitia Nicely climbed onto Pegasus, He was in one of his – fortunately - rare strops and had made his height a struggle for Miss Nicely at 5'3' to mount and then reach the pedals. Miss Nicely apologised for his inconvenience and for being abandoned in such an insensitive way, and murmured gently to him telling him how necessary and appreciated he was. A moment or two of this and Pegasus prepared for take-off and took to the sky.

With the realisation that she was going to have another encounter with the Hairy Coo. Miss Nicely turned Pegasus towards Glasgow and relaxed, enjoying the ride. The Hairy Coo, aka Angus Bulman was an unusual problem for Miss Nicely – he had no respect for her and was totally oblivious to her attempts to cajole him to reform and start living away from the criminal underground where he was quite the man. Miss Nicely saw a different side to the man. She was sure that if he just changed his ways, he could have a very good life without the criminality. In the meantime, she would keep talking to him and see what could be done to change his attitude. She had a final idea that she could try, but she wanted to see if he would respond to reason, at least another couple of times.

As Pegasus started to fly down towards the old docks where the Hairy Coo did his business, Miss Nicely spent a few moments thinking about the job ahead of her. Then she gave herself a small shake and as Pegasus landed, she prepared to dismount. She straightened her skirt and made sure that her hat was sitting right, and headed for the cabin where Angus had his office.

The Hairy Coo came out of the cabin to greet Miss Nicely.

'Well, you old busybody, so you couldn't keep away.'

'No Angus dear, I can't keep away when I know that you could be a so much better man than you are allowing yourself to be. I don't give up easily.'

'Well, you'll have your work cut out with me you old witch, no sorry I mean you ancient witch.'

`'Not a witch dear, more a superhero.'

'Well, a superhero, is it? I've never considered an elderly lady as a superhero before.'

'I assure you that that is what I am. I solve problems using my empathy and a stern word here and there. It's a good life. Particularly when I can see the good effects of my work, leaving peace and happiness behind me. Now someone like you tests my mettle and gives me a greater problem to get my teeth into.'

'Well, you elderly minx, I'll be providing you with a problem for a very long time.'

`'Thank you Angus dear, I appreciate your consistency, even though I wish you would put your mind to a life without crime.'

`'Well, thank you for that you redundant old besom, no, not redundant, redoubtable that's the word that I was looking for!'

'So, are you going to repent of your bad ways today dear? I would take just a little regret for one of your nefarious activities.'

'Well, nope – I guess I'll be staying the same old Hairy Coo. Now run along dearie, and let me get on scheming!'

There would be rain later, thought Miss Nicely as she mounted Pegasus and turned him towards her next stop. She had never been to Shipley before and understood it to be close to Bradford. She knew that it was a case of ill temper, and hoped that was all.

Pegasus landed in a row of dark stone terraced houses and gave Miss Nicely room to dismount on the pavement side, rather than in the road. She was very aware of the curtains twitching down the street. She checked the house number and, having made sure she was neat and tidy, rapped smartly on the door. A raging middle-aged man flung the door open and growled, 'What?'

'I've come about the bad temper dear,' responded Miss Nicely. 'I take it I'm speaking to Silas Shoesmith?'

'Yes, but what business is it of yours?'

'I am Miss Letitia Nicely, and I solve problems for a living. I've been made aware of your situation, and it is up to me to help to put things right. May I come in? We wouldn't want neighbours to become aware of your problems.'

'That's very true', grumbled Silas opening the door just wide enough to let Miss Nicely in.

The door led straight into the front room of the house.

Miss Nicely looked round and saw a tired looking middle-aged woman with four children round her.

'I take it that you are Jane Shoesmith? And these must be Annie, Edith, Rhodes, and Frank?'

'Yes, ma'am,' said Jane in some confusion. 'You aren't the social, are you? I do try my best for the children, but working in the shop all day exhausts me.'

'No dear, I'm not the social. My name is Letitia Nicely (Miss) and it's my job to help sort out problems before they get as far as the social. May I sit down?'

'Certainly ma'am,' replied Jane, moving a pile of ironing from a chair.

'Right,' said Letitia, 'I'd like to hear what's going on, in your own words. Silas, you go first Jane you will have your chance to speak, so let Silas have his say in respectful silence. Go ahead, Silas.'

'I am struggling with losing my sight, which is making it impossible for me to work in our greengrocery anymore. To keep the business going Janey is having to work all the hours God sends us, and that means that we are now missing the money that she used to bring in from her sewing. Our eldest son, Bertie, was looking good for university, but has had to leave school to earn another wage. He has a job in a local chip shop and is unfailingly good humoured about it and proud to hand his mother a pay packet at the end of each week. But I can't help feeling that I have failed my family, and that leaves me short tempered. I'm ashamed to say that I speak viciously and most unfairly to Janey. I seem to be worst on Bertie's payday. Janey, can you ever forgive me?'

'It's your turn now, Jane,' said Miss Nicely.

'You are an old silly, Silas Shoesmith,' started Jane with a sigh. 'Of course, I forgive you with all my heart. You didn't exactly decide to lose your sight - have you forgotten our wedding vows – in sickness and in health? I know that working on my own in the shop is exhausting, but I'm proud to keep going the business that you built up for us. I would have no respect for you if you had expressed no regret for our situation, and I too am sad that Bertie has had to give up his dream of going to university, but I'm proud of him for the way he is handling it. The only thing I would ask to be different about our situation is that you would stop shouting all the time. I understand your frustration and put up with it, but it runs the risk of breaking my heart and my spirit. I am doing my best for the family, and hate to be shouted at.'

'Well Silas, what do you have to say to Jane?' Letitia intervened.

'Oh Janey! I am so sorry that I've been taking my frustrations out on you, and now that I have heard you say that you are proud to work in our business, I don't have that to worry about any longer. I will make sure to tell Bertie how proud I am of him when he gets in from work tonight.'

'Now Silas, I am satisfied with what you have said to Jane. You won't hear from me anymore unless your behaviour becomes a problem again.' Miss Nicely was hopeful that having had a chance to be listened to Silas would be able to keep his temper better, although there would be slips of course.

She decided that she would just add a little zhush to the family to be on the safe side. The zhush as she thought of it, was a useful little booster for more difficult cases, and needed to be used with care and not at all if it was a case without a true penitent. It could be positively dangerous if used wrongly and was brought out only rarely as a result.

Miss Nicely opened the door and stepped out into the street. It would rain soon.

Miss Nicely was now able to turn Pegasus for home. She keenly anticipated her half an hour in her own cosy room, before she had to hand over to Vixen again. She hoped that she would now not be disturbed for the evening, and that it would be a quiet night too, she sometimes felt that she was getting too old for the night callouts, but she knew that secretly she loved her work whenever and wherever it took her.

The rain that had been threatening started now with a light drizzle. Letitia hoped that Pegasus would have her home before it properly set in. It was always dismal arriving home soaked through.

Very soon Pegasus started the descent to the yard belonging to the house that Vixen and Miss Nicely shared. He landed gracefully and allowed Miss Nicely to dismount before leaning himself on the adjacent wall.

Miss Nicely went into the house to be greeted by Creighton – the general factotum – and smiled when the latter said, 'Take yourself into the sitting room madam. I'll bring your tea and biscuits immediately.'

Miss Nicely was ready for that cup of tea and those biscuits. It had been a long day. The rain was now beating against the windows, and it was a good job that Pegasus had beaten it home. Otherwise, she would have been drenched.

Creighton came in with a tea tray. Miss Nicely made herself comfortable in her chair and gave a sigh of pleasure.

# Tidal waves

## Holly

The Moon is a puppeteer
Tide is its companion
Dragged through lows and highs
Battering coastlines
Vicious
unrelenting
Cliffs turned to dust
Each year
reclaiming
ground
seized by waves

# Detecting Dylan

## William Davidson

We go on a bat walk. Jenny gives out handheld bat detectors. Dylan says he doesn't need one. No doubt he's going to spot the bats to show off to Jenny, spot them with some kind of innate skill of night vision he'll claim to possess.

'These gizmos convert bat calls into audible clicks,' Jenny says. 'And if you hear a raspberry, that's a bat munching on an insect.' She blows a raspberry by way of demonstration.

We set out around the meadow and pause in a clearing in the woods.

'Common pipistrelle,' Dylan says.

A moment later, everyone's detectors start clicking.

Jenny points up at the dimming sky and says, 'Two of them. Two pipistrelles,' though I can't make them out. I think I blinked and missed them.

We walk to the cycle path just outside the reserve. Jenny says the bats like the streetlights because they'll find more insects to eat.

'There's another,' Dylan says but he's not looking up. He's actually got his eyes closed. Our detectors click like they're giving him a round of applause.

'Wow,' Jenny says. 'Good hearing.'

My detector emits a raspberry.

# Our House

## Samantha Bach

Farewell to you, Saint Bridget.
You were the walls
that kept me and mine safe
mostly…

Walls that at times felt
like a trap,
at times a safety net.
So many memories…

babies laughing, crying,
teenagers…
loud punk songs
kicking out at the world.

Often our house 'in the middle of the street'
was the youth club of extended family.
We laughed,
we cried at shared tragedies.

At times it all got too much…
I would shout and send off the crowds,
trying to claim or reclaim
my space, my home.

Our house in the middle of the street -
farewell Saint Bridget.

# Moogles McDermid and The Firefly's Bottom

**Lynne Parkin**

Moogles is sitting at her kitchen table, a piece of paper in front of her. She had been writing furiously and now that she has finished, she can send the letter to her dad in heaven by spell mail, but first she wants to make sure that she had written everything that is in her head and her heart.

Dear Dad,

Do you know how much it hurts that you left me, and how much I miss you? My heart is sore, and my mind wishes you were here every minute of the day and night. Now, everything I do is for you Dad. I know that you would be proud of me if you were here, and you would support me always. Mum hates everything I do, but that's nothing new is it dad? You are well rid of her, honestly you are. I just wish I could understand why you had to go without saying goodbye to me. Why you left me before telling me what to do without you. There wasn't even a goodbye hug or kiss, not even a wave. You didn't leave me a letter giving me the answers to all my questions, all the things a growing daughter and witch should know. I need you Dad and I have always needed you. I'm not at home now, because it wasn't a home without you in it. I left as soon as I could but not without a fight from her, I refuse to call her mother.

The treehouse we built in Noggins Wood, is now my forever home. I've upgraded it with a little magic and lots of help from Mr Noggins. He says I can keep it and use the wood as if it were my own. We've named the treehouse Owen's Den, I hope you like that dad, our place named after you. It has a kitchen, cosy room, and en-suite bedroom with observatory. I love looking at the night sky and looking for you. I'll never stop looking for you Dad. She doesn't know about the observatory, but she does know about the two cauldrons in the kitchen, and she doesn't like them and tells me so every chance she gets. One is full of never-ending soup and the other is used for potions and spells. The soup today is your favourite Dad, wild mushroom and garlic and for those who don't like it, it tastes like custard! I found one of the cauldrons on Mr Noggins' farm, he said it was one of yours.

Mr Noggins looks out for me, and he says he always will. He tells me stories about you both, the adventures you had, the things you got up to. It makes me happy listening to him, but also sad that we cannot do the same things. I can see why you became such good friends. You had so much in common. He brings Norman every day for a walk to see me. He ties him to the tree and comes up for a cup of tea. He doesn't like the dark like you dad and he hates mother. She hates his goat more than him, so she doesn't bother me when he is here. She can't reach me anyway, not with my retractable staircase. I do not see her as my mother anymore, she is not a nice person.

I've got to go now Dad. I'm sending you this by spell mail. Please, please reply so I can stop hurting inside.

Your loving Daughter,
Moogles

The wood, Noggins' Wood, belongs to Arthur Noggins, local farmer and landowner. He owns the wood and a two-acre small holding which comes with two chickens, Pearl and Ruby, two sheep, Daisy and Dandelion and a rather cantankerous goat called Norman who behaves like a spoilt puppy. He can be seen out walking daily in his plus fours, below the knee trousers to you and me, a string vest, tweed jacket and wellingtons. He also wears a monocle on important occasions, which shines in the sunlight. His daily jaunt always starts with putting Norman on his lead so they can visit Moogles McDermid in her tree house and this is where the story begins.

Moogles McDermid, witch to all things living, lives in a treehouse in Noggins' wood. Its whereabouts is only known by Farmer Noggins, his goat Norman and a few of her dad's friends who helped with the construction. Oh, and her mother, not that she has been inside, she has not. The wood has always been her playground and the treehouse her place to hide especially from her mother. Now as a grownup, she is seventeen after all, she has, with a little help from her magic, not just a safe place, it is the place she calls home. She lives alone, her dad died when she was young, and her mother does not agree with her lifestyle. But then her mother hasn't agreed with anything she has done throughout her life so far.

It has always been, 'No Morgan, you can't do this, you can't do that. You, become a witch, I don't think so!' She is so annoying. Her name is Moogles, her dad had always called her Moogles, everyone else calls her Moogles including Mr. Noggins, and her cat Autumn. So, at the earliest opportunity she moved out of her childhood home to her tree house. The one her dad, his friends and Farmer Noggins had built for her to play in. The treehouse turned from her childhood play retreat to her larger than average tree home. Her door is always open, unless it is her mother, then the stairs are raised rapidly.

Mr Noggins loves having a real witch living in his wood. She helps him with his aches and pains. Keeps him fed with her everlasting cauldron of soup and opens his eyes to the wonders of the wood. In the beginning her cat gave him the sneezes, but Moogles soon sorted that. Spirulina, stinging nettle, honey and a hair ball from Autumn the cat. She helped him when his chickens stopped laying, the potion had smelt disgusting and the words she had spoken sounded daft, but it worked. In fact, their egg laying tripled. Go Moogles!

Today, the Frost on the ground crunches underfoot, as Arthur Noggins walks haphazardly with Norman, towards the tree house. He has lots of things on his mind, which is nothing new. He was born a worrier and remains a worrier. The big issue he has in his life now is lack of sleep. He has a very noisy generator and cannot sleep without a light on, so he is in a vicious circle, of no sleep with light off, no sleep with the generator on. He arrives at the tree house has a good look round as he ties Norman to the tethering post; he must make sure he hasn't been followed by the enemy, Moogles' mother. Once he is sure he shouts up into the tree at Moogles' open front door. 'Morning Moogles, can I come aboard?'

She replies with a magic spell. 'From ground to treetop let him see, the stairs that will bring him up to me. Once inside again do hide until his descent is required.'

He climbs the stairs two at a time and smiles at the young lady in the doorway. She is dressed in purple with coloured rags in her hair and she is wearing clogs of the brightest green. Her cat Autumn, ginger the colour of the falling leaves, is asleep in a basket next to the log fire. She raises her head, acknowledges the newcomer's presence as friendly then goes back to sleep.

'Tea's ready, Liquorice root today,' she says and

smiles at Mr Noggins.

In the kitchen, they sit with mugs in their hands, swirling the hot liquid in them. They stare into their depths and Arthur sighs and sighs. Moogles frowns, she can see into his very soul.

'No Sleep?' she asks gently. Moogles knows all about his sleep problem. What a situation he finds himself in. At first, he kept quiet about his dilemma, he didn't like to bother Moogles with something so trivial.

'Hmm it's still a problem,' he mutters. Then he yawns a big wide air gulping yawn.

'I'm working on this,' she assures him. 'It won't be long now; it's just about putting the right spells together and I'm nearly there.'

Farmer Noggins smiles a big smile. 'I know,' he says. 'I am really grateful to you for trying.'

Farmer Noggins finishes his tea, gives Moogles a hug and leaves, but not before Moogles gives him some of her home-made donuts. They are especially for Norman. A mixture of meadow grass, watercress, honey, dandelion leaves and wheat flour. But Moogles knows Farmer Noggins eats them too, so she has made sure they are safe for them both to eat.

Now Moogles needs to focus on the spell to cure the lack of sleep.

'Dad where do I start,' she asks aloud. Turning to some of her dad's old spell and nature books, Moogles smiles. Of course, it is that simple she tells herself.

The following morning whilst they are drinking Lavender tea, Moogles pats Farmer Noggins on the arm. 'I have a solution.' She announces excitedly, 'One that is so clever, I wish I had thought of it sooner.'

'And that is?' he asks.

'This is so simple,' she says grinning. 'And it will work very well.'

From underneath her chair, Moogles brings out an object covered with a handkerchief. She places it on the table in front of Mr Noggins and with a flourish she reveals a jam jar. It is filled with what looks like dead bugs. Mr Noggins can't hide the disappointment on his face, but before he can say anything Moogles clicks her fingers, and the room goes dark. Instantly the tiny creatures wake up, they move quickly and lo and behold their bottoms light up. Their bottoms really light up the room.

'For your bedside table,' she smiles at him. 'And there is a carry handle. The glass itself is magic, it will keep the fireflies warm in winter and cool in summer. All that you need to do is feed them leaves and keep them clean.'

'Thank you Moogles,' Mr Noggins says, giving her a big hug. 'I knew you could do it. You are my very own private witch.'

'And you are my very special friend,' she replies.

The difference in Mr Noggins is apparent after only a few days. No more yawning or sighing. He is so happy that he has been into town and bought Moogles a large assortment of fancy ribbons for her hair. He is happy to treat his special friend.

# Easter

## Gareth Davis

the man was reborn
he died to save our souls
but what is a soul
are we just flesh and bone
or is there something more
why do we fall in love
just to self-destruct
what is life about
why are we here
good and bad
right and wrong
maybe it's better not to feel at all
but life without feelings is not living
that's what makes us human
god gave us free choice
the devil made beer

# River of Gold

## Cat Easterbrook

Once, there was a girl who was just a head. Not literally. That would be odd. No, no, she had a body. But the thing was, her head was enormous, so getting about was some trouble. She didn't much like to run or play. She'd crash and collide and fall all a wobble, so she sat real still and played in her head instead.

And oh wow what a playground she found. She'd spend all day roaming around, finding high mountain tops and hidden treasure troves, pirouetting white horses and a wild river goddess. The more time she spent there, the bigger the land got, and she would've just lived there if she could.

But in a place that everyone insisted on calling 'the real world' she lived in a house. It was really quite an ordinary house, a box of bricks, not much of note, but it was built on a slope, so everything was off kilter, just a bit, and with her huge head she noticed it. Her head became a scribble, a doodle and an anagram, a crossword with cryptic clues pointing to colourful far-off lands.

She sat, one day, heavy head in hands, looking out at a blank grey sky. I wonder if it's all just people in boxes out there? Or maybe there really is a wild river goddess? With this thought she felt a pull, like a magnet that pulled on her feet.

One day the magnet pulled her feet clean through the door. Her head followed reluctantly shouting, 'Where am I going?' No answer came but off she went on the feet she could barely feel, and when she reached the end of the street, she looked back at her box. It looked funny from here, like a made-up thing, and she could feel a tingling starting. The tingling was like her toes were dancing.

She reached the end of the boxes, the edge of her town. Her head said, 'What now? Call it a day?' But no, she decided to follow her feet, hoping they knew the way (because let's face it, her head certainly didn't).

As she walked the feeling grew, as tarmac turned to dirt then to grass. The feeling grew up her legs and they were tingling too. But the feeling was still so weak and her head felt far too big and bleak. She reached the riverbank and plonked it down on the stump of a tree.

A beady bird alighted next to her and seemed to laugh, and that made Harriet sinkingly sad. It wasn't her fault her head was so big. And yes, she knew she looked silly with it plonked on a tree but right now this was the only place she could be.

Harriet watched the shimmer of the river and down went the swelling in her head. What a funny thing that was, it seemed to shrink. And here was this feeling rushing up to her belly. And there it was a big breath like a bellow. Oh yes at this did she let out a chuckle.

Then her belly pumped some more. Big breaths blew her up like a balloon. She felt like she might just float away, into the sky of solid grey.... until her head shouted, 'What's happening!' and popped the balloon of her becoming.

Before she could try to float once more, a vole leapt from the shore with a splash. She thought they were shy, but not this guy, splishing and sploshing away. Harriet wanted to play like him, but she didn't know how to swim. A walk was enough to cause a wobble, so swim? Erm, no, absolutely not, no way. She left him there but first declared, 'I thought you were supposed to be shy!' And out of thin air came the reply, 'This guy ain't got time to be shy.'

She set off again, only to see someone kneeling at the river's edge, perhaps admiring their reflection, or panning the riverbed for gold instead. Harriet grew close and tried to speak, 'Hi' she managed to squeak.

'Hi, I'm Yuno, what do you like to be called?'

Harriet couldn't help but notice... Yuno's head also looked rather large and it bobbled about in a way that was happy and kind and perhaps a little bit sad but most of all it was kind and wow was their voice wild; it was from here, there and everywhere; a right old whistlestop tour of the world it was, anyway...

Yuno held out their hand for Harriet to shake. At this Harriet clean forgot her name, said nothing, shook nothing. Thankfully Yuno filled the silence with a smile, then said, 'Do you want to walk together a while?' Harriet's cheeks turned hot-sauce red and out tumbled some words, 'Oh yes, how nice, thank you please, let's.'

So off they set and as they chatted, the path grew tricky and strangely slippy. UGH did the two of them slip and slide. AGH it was all they could do to stay on their feet. EUGH did they want to quit. You bet ya they did. But instead they said, 'Let's help one another.' And that was a cure for their heads felt smaller and their steps grew steady and assured.

Around a curve in the riverbank, they came across a goat wearing a coat. This caused Harriet some consternation. Surely, this goat already has its own coat? As the goat met Harriet's eye, he was trying to scale a small hillock, and let's be honest, he looked like ... he was making a right palaver out of it.

'I thought climbing was supposed to be easy for a goat,' said Harriet to no one in particular- and no one in particular replied, 'Absolutely, yes, unless the goat has been bundled up in a duffle coat, in which case, no, not so much.'

Harriet wanted to help, but Yuno grabbed her and said, 'No, it's not your goat or your coat. Onwards.' Harriet went inwards instead and held a meeting with her head. Can Yuno really tell me what to do? Where do *I* want to go?

What do *I* want to do?

No answer came because she'd left behind that inner space the place that knows. The place with the pirouetting horses and the river goddess. She missed them. The missing made her sad and the sadness grew until there was a mighty crack in the middle of her body and it looked like she might just break in two.

'Uh oh,' said Yuno, producing all manner of accoutrements from their backpack: bandages and splints and plaster of Paris. Harriet was agape and agog at this. She raised one eyebrow askance at all the pushing and pulling and patching, and when Yuno stepped aside holding their hands ahigh as if to say, 'My work here is done,' Harriet thought, all well and good, but uf was it cumbersome to walk with such an apparatus.

And it was just at this moment that the crow was back and circling and cackling another horrid tune and the riverbank grew far too rocky and twisty and turny and she kept tripping and almost broke her ankle once or twice and near-on rolled into the river multiple times oh and a gale blew in and it was face-slappingly noisy with the wind and the rain and the crow and now her head was twice the size and the split was really coming apart at the seams and…

'…maybe just let it?' spoke a voice
'Just let it?'
'Yup.'
'Bu– but…I ca– ho– how do I let it?'
'You don't. You just let it.'

Well, that wasn't very helpful, she thought. This was followed by many other thoughts, before arriving at the simplest thought of them all, which was: ok.

Harriet sized up the crow and said, 'Ok,' but she didn't

cower, for she'd found some power inside of her. The crow cut through the air, fixing her with a deadly stare. And even though she wanted to hide, she looked him dead in his deadly eye. He stalled and came to land with a screech. Up close she could see his eye was kinda wonky.

'Oh no, poor crow, maybe he doesn't know where to go? I wonder if it's his eye that makes him so mean? Ok, my unlikely friend, you can stay, but you can't under any circumstances fly in *my* way.'

With crow alongside his tune began to change (not gonna lie, it was still pretty terrible) and the wind still blew but that breath like a bellow was back. And now too, her head was less of a scribble. Oh and did this feel better, clearer. This led her to raise a finger in the air, as if she had something really rather wise to declare. And here it came:

'I can feel the inside things and the outside things all together and all at the same time!' Which was a strange statement indeed and it had probably sounded better in her head.

Yuno laughed hard and fast before turning deadly serious to say, 'I know exactly what you mean.'

Harriet felt good to be understood, and the inside-out feeling grew as they walked the river's path. Inside and outside began to weave, until the river began to cleave a river right through her chest. A most unusual feeling, it was warm and flowing and silken too, slowly seeping out through a little split. At first she was afraid but then she relaxed, she let it.

In time the crack grew and oh did this feel dangerous. 'What if it starts to spill and doesn't stop? What a terrible mess I will make.' And remembering what a mess she'd had in her head, and in that box on the slope, she couldn't bear to let it flow.

Yuno stood by her side leaning sagely on a walking stick (that inexplicably they had, at some point, found the time to whittle) and they declared, 'A problemo this is not, for this is a wild river of old, a veritable river of gold.'

Harriet didn't know what this was supposed to mean, but she went with it, and her head scribbled a whole scene: 'What if the river of gold floods the land? What if the goddess rides the river of gold out to sea, never to be seen again? What if…?' she hung her head at what was to follow, 'What if the trolls and goblins and dragons use the river of gold to sweep out into the land then storm and stomp and stink away and basically wreck the joint?'

'Wow, you're being very dramatic, this evening,' said Yuno and gave Harriet a shove that wasn't without love, but it caught her off balance. Down she fell and oh did the crack in her chest burst open, with bandages unravelling and splints snapping, she bust out of the plaster of Paris and out flowed the river of gold, and with it rode beings from all of the worlds: pure white horses pirouetting, golden owls gliding, goblins and fiery dragons causing havoc and hoaxes, and in the centre of the chaos, rising from golden waters, a serene river goddess.

Even though she was afraid and in awe, Harriet welcomed them all the same, from goddess to goblin, for they were all part of her domain. She twirled with the horses, played tricks with the goblins, swam with the goddess, and flew with the owls. Walking had always been hard, but to fly? It's like she had always known how.

Yuno laughed and clapped at this parade of destruction and delight. But at points too they screamed and even got their hair singed by a dragon as it took flight. They stayed and never moved far, sometimes a clap of glee, a tear in their eye or a punch of the air, accompanied by the words: 'Pow, pow!' They also whittled their stick some more.

The stars shone bright that long, burning hot night.

There was light upon light upon light. Harriet's head grew bigger and bigger still. But now into her head, instead of all that consternation there appeared an almighty constellation. She flew through the stars so bright, until ... she really needed to get some sleep.

Harriet opened her eyes to the first signs of sunrise. She lay quivering a while her senses still so alive. She leapt to her feet, looked eagerly around, half-surprised to see the river not gold but green. And Yuno? Nowhere to be seen.

Harriet knelt at the river's edge, almost got lost in a shimmer and fell in. Where would she go without Yuno? But inside her chest was a feeling like liquid gold. A steady flow that let her know *exactly* where to go. For a moment she tried to ignore it, but no...it was time to go home.

Harriet leapt up, turned around and began to hurry. Now she knew the goddess and the owls she was invisible, unstoppable, no box would hold her back, she could fly and swim, she wasn't a scribble or an anagram, forget the consternation, she was an almighty constellation. She had a life to lead and she was ready to start right now.

Walking too fast and with her head in the stars, she didn't get far when she tripped on a rock and fell. Unbelievable. Barely two steps along the path and now face down in the grass. She cried out in pain and felt ashamed. Really? After all this, she was still just a mess?

Blinking back tears, her vision cleared, and there by her side was the stump of a tree. She squinted and slowly began to see a carving there, an unusual pair: a glorious goddess astride a golden dragon. The two of them serene as they leapt victoriously through the air.

Yes, this *can* be. This can be *me*. But I need to take things slowly and it's ok if I tumble from time to time, who knows what I might see right there in front of me? Harriet's head and heart said, a newly formed team.

The river carried her home and when she reached her town, the huddle of boxes, she looked around, seeing it anew. It wasn't just her box that was skewwhiff. All the boxes were wonky at least a bit. The wonky huddle made her heart grow and the river of gold flow and flow.

And her box on the slope? She made it her own, a place to call home, with kind-hearted friends all around. And that mysterious place of inner space, the wild river goddess and pirouetting horses? She didn't need to hide them now. Just like her adventure had shown her how, she slowly let them out, released from a too-tight space, to unfurl and uncurl and live in the world, and she rode alongside with a pow.

# Surf Collage

## Georgia Conlon

We yearn
for the sisterhood of the sea:
a sensorial existence
shared with the ocean
and all her alchemy.

Take off, then soul arch –
fade into the depths.
Clouds that escape
your mouth
between swells and storms
are incomprehensible,
eclipsed by peace
within chaos.

Wave-lashed, rhythmic,
surf-hungry,
the ocean's water sisters
are painted euphoric,
transformed in deep autonomy.

Under lips of firing waves
our souls swallow the horizon.

Torrential days are never eternal.

# Dragon Fire

## James Wilson

*James dedicates this story to his cousin Simeon who passed.*

## Prologue

*In the outreaches of the world there is a mountain range surrounded by forest. It has been said for the past 100 years that a dragon lives in a cave within the mountain range. The mountain range has many caves and snow-peaked tops. Water runs down from the top of the mountains, droplets pouring down at the entrance to the dark caves.*

*Below the mountains is a village made up of wooden huts with great strips of wood forming the sides of the huts. They have wood burners inside encased in iron covered fire with iron and with an iron pipe to the roof to let the smoke drift away into the starlit skies.*

*There have been various sightings of the dragon by local villagers and by the townsfolk who went to see their family in villages.*

## PART ONE

The dragon had been described as long, thin with enormous wings and jet-black eyes and to be a greenish-brown colour with a hint of red. One townsman said he had seen the dragon flying across the mountains and letting out a fierce stream fire. But the villagers said this was hocus-pocus and the townsman was drunk and delusional. That night the mentioned villager had stumbled home after much laughter from the villagers. He had told his wife and she had listened intently. He believed he knew what he saw and that morning he had sketched a charcoal drawing of the dragon, but he rolled it up and hid it in a chest under their bed so as not to be ridiculed by the villagers.

The next day two of the villagers, Edwin and Ester, decided they would make their way to the mountains to see if the tales of a dragon were true. The villagers had by this time named the dragon Dragonfire. Edwin brought the horses round, and they filled the saddle bags with supplies. Edwin had a sword his uncle the blacksmith had given him with a sheath and a strap so it was fastened to his back. Ester had oils and ointments which she put in her horse's saddle bag. These were meant to be able to heal wounds but at the age of twenty-one she had not needed to use them yet. Ester had long brown plaited hair and blue eyes. She wore fabric trousers and a blue top that matched her eyes. Edwin had brown hair too, his short, and had a thick coat, padded at the shoulders with a chainmail jacket. He wore a pair of boots his uncle had given him.

Ester's horse was grey and Edwin's black. They rode quickly through the heavy rain as they wanted to make camp at the base of the mountains by nightfall.

As they got closer to the mountains there was a bridge across a stream. The stream was running fast with the water splashing hard against the rocks at the banks of the river. The water was dark blue with hints of green from the foliage that had fallen in. The bridge was stone, crumbling in places with stone supports each side. It had grand rectangular stone tops at each end.

Edwin thought he saw a creature move out of the forest near the bridge.

Ester said, 'We must take care whatever it is out there that's going to hinder us crossing the bridge.'

They got closer to the bridge, and Edwin could make out

a creature that looked like an ogre. He drew his sword and ordered Ester to stop. He dismounted from his horse, his boots creaking in the mud. The Ogre had claws and fat green flesh and a howl like a wolf. Edwin knew he had enough skill with a sword to pass the ogre. He shouted, 'We will cross the bridge!'

The ogre swiped at Edwin with its claws but was slow and clumsy. Edwin stumbled backwards. A thin trickle of blood ran down Edwin's chainmail. Edwin struck the ogre with a side swing of his sword and wounded the ogre. The ogre tried to get footing again on the bridge but its fat stubby legs giving as it almost fell back. The ogre, tall in stature, hit one of the rectangular tops on the bridge; with the size of the ogre, the stone top crumbled and crashed into the river, hitting the water hard and getting washed downstream. To the right was a dark, thick, overgrown forest with gnarly branches and a dark mist surrounding it. The ogre started to run back away to the forest and Edwin got back on his horse and called to Ester. 'We will cross!'

They both galloped across the bridge. It was long with stone barriers each side and ran towards the mountains. The mountains were usually surrounded in mist and it was only at sunrise when there was much light surrounding them.

## PART TWO

As Edwin and Ester rode towards the mountains in search of the dragon, Dragonfire, they came across another person on the path: a prophet called Zarl who was dressed in a black velvet gown with a shawl hood. Zarl the Prophet was holding a crystal ball in each hand. She was stood in a clearing with the remains of an abbey in the distance. But little remained of it. More crumbing stone ruins.

Edwin recognised her and greeted her, 'Hello Zarl, what news do you bring?'

The crystal balls started to glow and Zarl said, 'Beware when you get to the mountains. There is talk of a snow yeti there.'

Ester said, 'Will he let us pass?'

Zarl walked towards Ester and put one of the crystal balls into her saddlebag.

Zarl said, 'It's unlikely, but with the crystal ball you should be able to create a heat that will stop him in his tracks.'

Edwin and Ester got close to the mountains and decided they would make camp. The sun was beginning to go down but it left a trail of amber colours in the sky. Spots of rain were beginning to trickle down. They dismounted the horses and tied them up, then took off their saddle bags and lit a small fire. In Edwin's saddle bag he had a fabric sheet. They collected long strong sticks and made a shelter – draping the fabric over the framework of the sticks. The fire was very warm. Also in Edwin's saddle bag was a joint of ham and some rice. They prepared their food and kept warm by the fire. Edwin kept his sword by his side. Ester had her bow and the crystal ball in her satchel bag close by.

The next morning Edwin and Ester got the horses ready and packed up camp. They were close to the mountains now where Dragonfire the Dragon is said to be.

The high tops of the mountain had a crisp covering of snow, and the rock was mossy green in patches. There were cave entrances at different places, visible dark gaps in the rock across the mountains.

They rode off and after an hour or two reached a clearing. They were almost in the open.

Edwin scanned across the path ahead, but he saw nothing.

Then Ester said,' Did you hear that?'

Edwin heard a yowl and drew his sword. 'I think it's the yeti the prophet spoke of.'

Carefully, Ester drew the crystal ball from her saddle bag and placed it on her saddle.

She also drew her bow and poised an arrow.

Across the path a big creature - the snow yeti, covered in snow - blocked their path. Ester fired three arrows: one hit his chest, the other his head and one his leg. The Yeti let out a howl. Edwin dismounted his horse and slashed at the yeti with his sword. As the Yeti fought, he endured wounds and his blood dripped, dark in the soft white snow. Skilfully missing the Yeti's swipes, Ester held the crystal ball, which was letting off light and heat. She was glad of her leather gloves as it got hotter and hotter.

The yeti retreated.

Quickly, Edwin and Ester got back on their horse and raced up to the mountain.

## PART THREE

Edwin and Ester were getting high into the mountains, close to the cave where the dragon Dragonfire was said to be. Each cave entrance looked eerily dark with shadows and little light breaking into them. At this point they tied up their horses and continued on foot. Edwin had his sword fastened to his back and Ester had her bow. They finally reached the entrance to the cave. There were overgrown green vines around the entrance and the trickle of water coming from higher up in the mountains. They did not know and could not tell if the dragon was there.

It was silent.

Edwin pulled a branch from a tree and made a torch and lit it.

Edwin and Ester entered the dark of the cave. The water droplets from above poured down. Underfoot there was thick mud and they had to pull foliage away to enter. They trod carefully and descended, deep, deep down into the lair of Dragonfire.

Edwin could make out a shadow of a creature which they knew would be the dragon. The shadow looked huge on the cave wall, showing the outline of its wings. In the darkness with the torchlight burning down slowly the dragons head looked like nothing Edwin had seen before.

They stopped.

The dragon was real. They turned round and ran. Trying to get their footing in the thick mud on the base of the cave, Ester lost her footing, stumbled, and Edwin tried to pull her up. But the dragon was awakening. Dragonfire breathed burning hot fire and a piercing roar. Edwin and Ester began to run, but the dragon began to fly and clawed at them with his talons. Edwin tried to fight his way free but it was useless. The Dragon talons were sharp and blood- stained, and the grip on Edwin and Ester was phenomenal. Edwin had dropped the burning torch and tried to get a grip on his sword, but it was hopeless.

The dragon flew out of the cave, its huge wings opening like nothing Edwin had known, with Edwin and Ester struggling to get free. Out of the darkness of the cave and into the daylight, Dragonfire went onto the mountain top - a thin outcrop with sun shining across the ice - and dropped Edwin and Ester there. He perched above them on a mountain ledge and spoke with a deep roar of a voice, but it sounded tattered and fragile. 'Who are you?'

Edwin said, 'Edwin and Ester.'

The dragon asked, 'Where do you come from?'

Edwin said, 'The village. We mean you no harm, and you really have done nothing wrong at all'. At this point the Dragon took flight and flew to the darkness of the cave again. Dragonfire's huge wings folded as his talons slid in the wet mud at the entrance to the cave.

Edwin and Ester couldn't quite believe it. They started to descend the mountain to the safety of their horses. They were a bit confused that Dragonfire, despite breathing fire and seeming so ferocious, seemed to be gentle. Or had they been deceived?

They knew the villagers would be eager for their return and the news about how gentle Dragonfire was.

Edwin and Ester climbed on their horses and rode quickly. The rain was pouring down and the path treacherous. The ride home would be tough.

# Director's Cut

## Samantha Martin

If the movie of your betrayal were true
I'd understand - it was unplanned...
I guess I expected a skirmish, not a slaughter
No sign of war, no flags, no deep waters...
But
Directors Cut...
A different scene unfolded
You were far away
Emboldened

I'll see who I want!
I'll get what I want!
I'll do what I want!
You can't change me!

Meanwhile, I'm high in the hills
Paying the bills
Lost in the blink of a screen
Month after month
paying to see the end of my dreams
Lucky 13th
No rest, no reprieve from that final scene...

My cards on the table, yours up your sleeve
Why so brutal, why so cruel?
My agony
was it your fuel?
It takes my breath away, the poison I took each and every day

I flayed myself with your hate
using strips of my soul to stem the bleeding
Finally retreating

to a dark

hellish-hole…

Digging through the ground and your story
There were no moments of glory
Just sadness
and madness

two stories...

# Sapphire Eyes

## John F. Goodfellow

Sapphire Eyes dance and glisten

To me, make me simile.

What is it all metaphor, this soft feeling inside of me,

That makes my heart skip a beat where once you sat?

Like a cat stretched out charming me with your open heart and head-back

Laughter?

Where once my mind was blank, let's be frank,

All I can think of

Is

Your Sapphire Eyes.

# End of the World

## Kai-Latifa Hunter

It was the end of the world. Well, in fifteen minutes and twenty-six seconds, it would be the end of the world. Ella sat on the beach watching the sunset for the final time. On her lap lay her trusty companion, Louis, who purred softly as her fingers ran through his soft ginger fur. The sky was a beautiful eclectic mix of orange and pink hues. The sea crashed against the sand, creating a striking concert of sounds for the pair to listen to. Ella looked at Louis and smiled, happy to enjoy their last moments together.

The last year on Earth was a hectic time. Scientists had discovered their timeline for the Sun becoming a red giant was slightly off, give or take a few billion years. Luckily, the brightest minds were on the job, and they found a solution. For once, humanity was at peace; countries previously at war shared resources, and political parties worked bipartisanly, all for the common goal of finding a solution. All it took to save humanity was the end of the world. When it was announced that scientists had found a new solar system with a planet similar enough to Earth, humanity cheered. The next day people celebrated in the streets, hugging their neighbours. Gigantic spaceships were built around the world; governments organised transport for all citizens so they could board the metal birds. People packed their lives into single suitcases as they prepared themselves for the new world. Every day until the spaceships took off, there was a countdown on every television, radio and phone, signalling their imminent departure. Ella celebrated the departure with the bottle of rum she had been previously saving for a special occasion. She never knew what special occasion she was saving it for, but this seemed like it fit the criteria. Louis celebrated with a saucer of catnip tea and had a pretty good night himself. The next day Ella packed her and Louis's belongings and then went to Louis's pre-departure appointment. After the appointment, Ella got the bad news, Louis wouldn't be allowed to board. He had cancer. The vet apologised profusely but told Ella they had no room for dying pets, who would only be a drain on resources. Ella decided against boarding the ships and resolved to stay with her only family. She couldn't leave Louis to die alone. Three days later, the ships took off, and the earth fell silent as if aware of its imminent demise.

The next countdown started. The end of the world. Fifty four days, six hours, twenty eight minutes and fifty four seconds.

Ella and Louis spent the next few months relishing each other's company. The pair spent many nights in front of the fireplace. Louis would curl up in the old armchair, his eyes fixed on Ella as she twirled around the living room floor to the powerful voice of Etta James. During the days, Ella swam in the sea, exploring the underwater world that flourished below her. Louis spent the days running and rolling across the sand. The pair ate like royalty, with a feast for every meal.

On the final day, 12 hours, 16 minutes and 37 seconds, Ella prepared the pair a picnic. She brought out all the pillows and blankets she could find down to the shore and laid them out. On top of the blankets, she placed the picnic basket, her CD player, and a picture of her parents. That day Etta James could be heard for miles. The pair enjoyed their picnic spread periodically throughout the day and cuddled up amongst the pillows and blankets as evening drew upon them. Louis burrowed his head against Ella's belly and waited patiently for the strokes to begin.

58 minutes and 29 seconds, the CD player died.

37 minutes and 3 seconds, a flock of birds flew across the

sky in an almost liquid state.

19 minutes and 48 seconds, a pod of whales swam by, saying hello from their blowholes.

15 minutes and 26 seconds, Louis purred loudly, and Ella reminisced over the past year.

1 minute. Ella pulled Louis close, giving him a big hug. Louis snuggled up against her. The sky swirled a symphony of colours; the end was near. Ella noted how beautiful the end looked. As the seconds ran out, Ella closed her eyes and dug her face into Louis's fur for comfort. They were at peace, and so was the world.

# seasonal difference

## Paul Francis Wort

In this wood
where once there was
almost unbearable heat,
there is now
damp, sodden cold
and a different face of nature
reveals itself
to the daylight.

Fewer animals are venturing out

and we wander
in a different way now

and things are bare
and displayed now

in a way they weren't before

when they were cloaked
in leaves
and summer haze
and pollen
and insects
and noise
and hiddenness
and mystery

yet we still get lost… you and I.

And then I see you were right
about the way back
to the path home

but I say nothing
and keep battling through the undergrowth.

# Little Miss Annalise: From Birth to Adolescence

## Ann N

*This story is about childhood memories, based on the true life of the author. Names, dates and locations have been changed.*

Annalise was born in the hot Summer of 1976 at night time. Her parents, Jeany and Johnny, lived in a village, four miles away from Darlington town centre. Darlington is a town in County Durham in England. Jeany and Johnny's baby didn't weigh much at all and looked like a doll, because she was so tiny. Annalise was born with lower limb abnormalities and her legs turned inwards from the knees downwards.

Jeany and Johnny first met at a Dance Hall in Darlington and got married a few years later, in 1969 and were very pleased to welcome their long-awaited baby.

The pram for Annalise was an old-fashioned Silver Cross, which was blue with a chrome frame. Jeany enjoyed taking Annalise out and about and sometimes went to the local river, to feed the ducks. Also, Jeany and Johnny took Annalise to a nearby beck to feed the ducks, where there was a playground and tennis courts too.

Johnny worked in the Building Industry as a Quantity Surveyor and Jeany worked in a High Street Chemist store as an Assistant and also worked in a bank in the town centre of Darlington and they both worked very hard to earn money, so they could have a secure and happy life and afford to go on holidays too.

Jeany was a stay-at-home mother after Annalise was born and enjoyed cooking and baking. She made her own Christmas cake each year, using her mother's recipe. Annalise enjoyed licking the contents of the bowl.

In 1980, Jeany and Johnny welcomed baby number two and named her Catherine. She was born mid-morning and had lovely dark hair.

In 1981, Annalise started Infant School, which was a short distance away from home, with her best friend Sally who lived in a house directly opposite Annalise's. In the School playground was a climbing frame and some benches.

Annalise enjoyed story time and playing in the wendy house in the school hall. At lunchtime, when Annalise wasn't able to go home, she ate with the other pupils in the school hall. She was a slow eater and often the dinner ladies would move Annalise to a side table, to let her finish eating her packed lunch, so the dinner ladies could clean and tidy up.

Sally and her parents, Mavis and Rory, moved from Bridlington to Darlington when Sally was around four or five years old, and she was an only child.

Annalise and Sally played with dolls and toys, under the car port in Sally's driveway, whenever they had chance to meet up and play outside.

During their childhood, Annalise and her sister Catherine both enjoyed having birthday parties and also attending friends' birthday parties. Due to their age difference and not attending school at the same time, they each had a different set of friends.

In preparation for their birthday parties, Jeany took her children into town to choose a birthday cake for them and Annalise found it really fascinating, when the cake shop had pages and pages of designs to choose from, of pictures to go on to a cake.

Annalise attended Junior School and one of her favourite teachers was Mr Scott, who had a very good sense of humour, and he made lessons more enjoyable to be a part of.

She enjoyed going on school trips and in year three of Junior School, Annalise went to Preston Park in Stockton on Tees. Sometime, whilst at Junior School, she went with her class to the Trout Farm in Pickering, North Yorkshire.

When Annalise and her class were in the final year of Junior School, she found out that her best friend Sally was not planning on being educated at the Secondary School that Annalise was going to and was also moving to a different Borough of Darlington, with her parents.

Away from School, both Annalise and Catherine went to Piano lessons on a Saturday morning. Catherine was awarded a few Grades for her effort, but Annalise didn't do so well as she found it difficult to read music and had small hands.

They both went to Gymnastics and Annalise went to Brownies and Guides in her local village church hall.

Johnny's parents, Harold and Muriel regularly visited Johnny and family on a Saturday and Harold drove his car until he was elderly. Harold and Muriel lived a few miles away, in a different Borough of Darlington.

On a Sunday, Annalise and her family regularly went to Scarborough for the day, and walked down to the seafront, where their favourite fish and chips restaurant was. They ate inside and chatted to the staff who remembered them.

Annalise and Catherine enjoyed playing on the beach with a ball and visiting the amusement arcades.

Christmas time was traditionally spent at home. On Christmas Eve, Annalise and her Family went to a Church in the town centre of Darlington, to sing Christmas carols.

Jeany invited her Stepfather Leslie and her Grandad Jack to join her family at home, for Christmas Day dinner. They all ate prawn cocktail and salad for starters before the Christmas dinner, which included turkey, pigs in blankets and plenty of vegetables.

As Annalise got older, no one bought her a diary for Christmas, which made her feel sad.

On Boxing Day, it became a tradition to visit Johnny's sister Gertrude and her husband Fred, who had two daughters called Ermentrude and Gladys. They lived in Newcastle Upon Tyne.

Occasionally Harold and Muriel would travel to Newcastle earlier in December, to spend more time with their daughter and her family, so they would already be there for the Christmas festivities, by the time Annalise and her family arrived on Boxing Day.

They would all enjoy a second Christmas dinner together, with at least ten people sitting around a huge table. After dinner, Gertrude used to play the piano and Ermentrude used to play her flute.

Annalise often felt really nervous, travelling as a car passenger and socialising, even with people she knew well.

Just after Boxing Day, Jeany's half-sister and family visited Jeany and everyone enjoyed talking, opening presents and playing Christmas games. Johnny would buy a few cans of beer in for the occasion, and fizzy drinks for the children. There were nuts, crisps and an open fire to enjoy.

# Hedged In: The Reluctant Cyclist

## Olya Bowers

The hedges were too tall so I could see nothing of the South Downs from my bicycle. Last time I was here I was hitch-hiking. The rides in lorries then gave me panoramic views.

The mystery was how had this bloke, Paul, convinced me to do a cycling holiday, complete with tent? He was leading the way but seemed always out of sight and I was left trapped in a tunnel of hedge on a one-lane road. Every blind corner I expected to meet the Grim Reaper. There was no shoulder to pull over on – it was all hedge, hedge, hedge, good for birds to nest in and hedgehogs to rummage but not favourable to cyclists. Paul had informed me that these 5000-year-old swine-herder trails were nobly worn down through the ages, but I found myself being worn down ignobly yet feigning enthusiasm in order to impress this man. If I wasn't so terrified, I could ponder and perhaps realise how pathetic my man-pleasing behaviour is, but my forte is denial, preferable to self- analysis.

I told Paul on Date.com that I was a keen cyclist. I wasn't completely lying as I did now own a bike left behind by Pamela in lieu of the rent she owed. And I was keening for love with a lustful, but not cycling, component. To his credit, Paul got all the camping gear together and kitted my bike with rack, panniers, bell, lights and covered my body with reflective gear. He obviously did not wish me dead, though I feared that might come later. If the relationship ended, as these things usually do, I hoped he'd opt for texting me and not choose femicide.

Snaking and slithering along death-trap roads is perfect for mindfulness. I had never felt so in the moment, my thoughts never strayed, my hands continuously poised over the brakes, my calves and thighs hot and throbbing, though not from pleasure. My spine, in screaming its pain, annoyed me because I needed to focus on swerving past the Grim Reaper.

The cheerful disposition I had displayed to Paul did not prove to be resilient when the rain swept in horizontally, drenching me and making the swineherder's trail very slick. I reminded myself how good moisture is for the skin, and how lucky I was not to be actually walking through the countryside, so full of Lyme-disease-carrying ticks. The rain became more exuberant at beating my face and filling my shoes. It was accompanied by a wind which made forward motion problematical. They say that misery loves company, but I had none. Paul seemed to have disappeared on his own watery adventure.

At that point the bladder I had successfully ignored intimated that evacuation was imminent. I pulled up by a farm gate and entered Lyme disease territory, exposing my disease – free buttocks to hungry ticks. I presumed Paul was far away by now, though to be truthful, I could hardly remember him.

But he hadn't forgotten about me. He skidded up to the gate and caught me en-flagrante or alfresco or whatever foreign word it's called. He looked like a bi-pedal drowned rat, but I was in no position to criticise.

'You're mooning me a bit early in the game, aren't you?' Paul quipped.

Witty retorts elude me, unless in retrospect. I groaned, and then I moaned as I discovered that the size 10 cycling shorts that I'd optimistically purchased, refused to pull up over my wet bum. I had so wanted to fulfil his request for a fit, athletic woman who loved all outdoor activities. I had even agreed to fly fishing. He'd packed an extra rod for me but I hate fish, so scaly and slimy, their smell so pungent—

and their flesh brings me out in hives.

I tell my friends that the human attribute I most admire is authenticity. I often declare righteously that I hate phoney people. 'With me, what you see is what you get!' Yes, that's correct, hypocrisy is my middle name. Of course, my bloke doesn't know that yet. Yes, he sees me. And what he gets is me, tipped over in the mud, arse up in the air.

I once had a boyfriend who told me that incompetence is not a turn on, so, unless this bloke was kinky about mud and freezing rain, my amorous skills were about to fail again. Not that I was interested in seduction at this point. Survival and escape were on my mind now.

As I pulled at my shorts, my mind tripped down memory lane, crossing the Mackenzie River in spate. I couldn't seem to exercise control over anything.

'Be careful, the river is in spate,' said the bloke I was trying to charm five years ago. He'd equipped me with dungaree waders and flyrod. 'Don't let the water go over the top as your waders and boots will fill and you'll be swept downstream. We lose a few fishermen this way every spring.'

His words hardly put a spring in my steps over slippery rocks whilst persistent currents swirled around my waist as I tried to reach the distant bank of the river. Fear was a propellant, but did not aid balance nor my gait, ungainly enough on dry land. I waved the fishing rod from side to side, recalling that long sticks help tightrope walkers. Yes, I survived, though the relationship didn't, nor my passing passion for fishing.

Wet hands tucked at my hips then around my pudgy belly, bringing me back to my rude predicament. I was half naked, yet I had hardly even kissed Paul. I remembered that my fisherman had liked my soft peasant body, but in this situation, with my skin-tight size -10 shorts, I had tried to project athleticism. This time I had definitely been caught out with my knickers down.

I'd love to claim that hot passion transcended mud and rain and a steamy session ensued but no, it was simply embarrassing as he lurched me upright and I covered my exposed pudenda. 'What a lovely word, pudenda' I said. A very wet Paul looked puzzled. I suspected he was in no mood to expand his vocabulary.

'Do they have monsoons every year in Kent?' I asked, and then started chattering – or rather my teeth did. I shivered and shook, but not with excitement.

'Bloody hell, at this rate you'll get hypothermia,' he said.

Paul hoiked me over to a tree and plonked me down. He returned to his bicycle to get his pannier and pulled out a fleece and a flask.

'Here, let's take off your wet jacket and shove your arms through this fleece.'

From the flask came the comforting smell of coffee.

'Drink this.'

I spluttered. 'Ugh—It's sweet, I don't like sugar.'

'Drink it —you need sugar now.'

Next from his pannier emerged one of those crinkly silver space blankets. He wrapped it around me. Tears as well as raindrops ran down my cheeks. I brushed them aside. I saw streaks of mascara on the back of my hand, providing proof of my now ghoulish face. I wished I was dead, but I followed his orders and drank that too-sweet coffee.

Paul bustled efficiently around me. He put waterproof trousers on my legs and force-fed me flapjacks, ruining my X-Factor diet. He removed his soggy jacket and crawled under the space blanket pressing his toasty chest into my ice-boxed breasts. 'I hope I'm not being too forward, but this has to be done.' He clasped me tightly and his hot breath on my neck made me feel human again. I realised this was what I truly wanted, to let go, to be carried, not for life but for a little bit of every day. I was tired of trying to be grown-up and attempting competence 24 hours a day. People found me funny, said I was good company, but life wasn't a joke. Hypothermia is real in so many ways and I had frozen out important parts of myself. Was I now ready to melt and was this man willing to drink all of me, whether alkaline or acidic. Was I brave enough to be truly authentic?

I wasn't chattering now. I was babbling and blubbering. Paul whispered 'Hypothermia is disorientating. You can even have hallucinations, but don't worry, you'll soon be back to normal.'

But normal was not where I wanted to be.

# Responses to Feminism

In 2021 and 2023 Converge ran a course called 'An Introduction to Feminism'. The course explored the history and activities of the Feminist movement from Hildegard of Bergen to the present day.

At the end of each session the group were invited to respond creatively to that week's material, in any medium they wished. Works of drawing, dance, collage and crochet were created as a result, along with a panoply of writing, some of which is included here.

We hope it inspires you!

# Rapunzel

## Karen Wilson

I'm leaning out of the window having a fag. I look down. I can see him way down there at the foot of the Tower shouting up at me. I send him a WhatsApp: '*i can't hear a word you're saying*'. He replies '*Let down your hair, I'll come up to rescue you*'.

*Illustration by Karen Wilson*

If that prick thinks he's putting his full weight on my scalp and dragging himself up here he can fuck right off. And what makes him think I want to leave anyway? I like it here, I'm happy on my own, and no one can come in to tell me what to do or mansplain my life to me.

I'll stay up here thanks, and I'm getting my hair cut anyway.

# Discovery

## Anda

You weaved some magic over me,
I can not let you go now.

Just finished this sensual interlocking and sending those inner bells gong.

And that is a quite of discovery.
With the note ... saying, do not disturb, in her eyes.

# Feminism Wordsearch

## Kate Hignett

```
      S E X I S M
    M E T O O * M V
  G *             A W
  E                 G C
P N                   H U
E D                   I N
R E                   L E
I R                   D Q
O *                   B U
D S                   I A
S T                   R L
  E                   T
  R E               X H
    O T Y P E S * S E
      P A Y * F G M
            F
            E
            M
        V O I C E
            N
            I
            S
            M
```

# We Will Be Quiet No Longer

## Naomi Nunns

Don't give them knowledge
Don't give them power
Silence and quiet them
Keep them in their place

These women of value, these women of change
Challenging misogyny since the early days
Too easily a danger to men's power and authority
Don't dare educate them or given them a voice

But we won't stay silent to your oppression and abuse
We'll be seen and we'll be heard
Because we're just the same as you
We'll fight to stand on equal ground
To Learn
To Write
To Vote
To Work
To choose how we live OUR lives

For all these things, and more

We will be quiet no longer.

# Symbol of Oppression

## Virginia Sellar-Edmunds

Oppressed – depressed
Forlorn, careworn but careless – bra-less.
Cast off the symbol of oppression (and compression)
Let the world see me as I am – a plump frump

Choose between conformity and deformity, or freedom.
Still, they say, the old ones - 'you'll go all to pot' - what rot.
See look at me! I'm free!

But no! You share your view with me,
Freely, gladly; and I love you,
So, sadly I'll reform, conform.
It's time to return to the land of the living.
Giving you a wife, whose shape shows hope.
Roped, lassoed, corralled.
A boost to my morale – and more?
Now as once before, tamed but maimed.

With hope I'll cope.
Although,
Women were not made so.

*Previously published by Heypressto (1998)*

# Thanks to You

## Helen Kenwright

I don't know how old I was when I first heard the word 'suffragette'. It's a word I've always known, somehow. Like 'engine' and 'washing-up'. It was a household word. My great aunt had been a suffragette. My mum taught me that suffragettes were brave women who fought for women's rights. I knew who they were long before I even realised the patriarchy existed. It was on TV, too, with an emphasis on the brutality of punishment rather than a celebration of the women who sacrificed so much for what they believed in.

I thought they were awesome.

Over the years I've found stories, names and lives beyond the Pankhursts. Many of the suffragettes seem eccentric, different, creative. Barefoot dancers, pipe smokers, monacle-wearers. Outspoken, imaginative, determined. People out of step. Perhaps all revolutionaries are.

Certainly, the best people are.

There's so much I couldn't do if it wasn't for the suffragettes and those who followed. I have independence some of my heroines could scarcely dream of. I have been able to live a life in learning and helping others to learn. I've been a campaigner on the front lines of protests and marches, and a campaigner in the back lines of media and speeches and press and everyday conversations.

We stand on the shoulders of giants. Generation by generation, we grow taller.

I always vote. I've been a member of the Green Party for over twenty-five years, so it's rare that my vote goes to the winning side. But I can't be accountable for anyone else's choices. The important thing is that I have the right to make my own.

I always say a little 'thank you' to the suffragettes when I cast my vote. But! 'Words, not deeds!' they insisted. Tricky to tackle when your main skill in life is writing.

But I try.

**General election 2001: Selby[6]**

| Party | Candidate | Votes | % | ±% |
|---|---|---|---|---|
| **Labour** | **John Grogan** | **22,652** | **45.1** | **−0.8** |
| Conservative | Michael Mitchell | 20,514 | 40.8 | +1.7 |
| Liberal Democrats | Jeremy Wilcock | 5,569 | 11.1 | −1.0 |
| Green | Helen Kenwright | 902 | 1.8 | *New* |
| UKIP | Graham Lewis | 635 | 1.3 | +0.3 |
| | **Majority** | 2,138 | 4.3 | -2.5 |
| | **Turnout** | 50,272 | 65.0 | −9.7 |
| Labour **hold** | | **Swing** | | |

[Table from news.bbc.co.uk]

*Courage calls to courage everywhere,*
*and its voice cannot be denied.*

- Millicent Fawcett

# What Writing is to Me

## Converge Creative Writing Class of '23

*This is a group poem created by students across all our Creative Writing classes in summer 2023.*

The thought of spreading joy, made real
Keeping your creative spirit alive
Gives me the element of surprise like sitting on a hedgehog
Escape to a hidden world that I constructed
Expressing myself through word artistry
The difference between near and far
A chance to bring alive the creative mind

The flow of the pen and what appears on the page
To have a pen in my hand is to let both live purposefully; the flowing fusion of ink and blood spills and an inner peace is restored

Writing helps me express my frantic and ambitious mind
Writing brings peace

Writing is creating and completing an experience
Writing means I haven't lost my grip on life
Writing is being imaginative and not losing my creativity
Writing is wide-awake dreaming

Writing is my core, like lettering on a stick of seaside rock
Writing helps me to show people who I am
Finding a freedom and philosophy and a space to be me

Writing is exploration and adventure
A freedom for my mind and an escapism from time

Community, companionship and blissful solitude
Communal and individual
Writing is a way of connecting with other people
Writing is like holding hands

Writing is a buzz, a warmth, a kind of light

Writing empowers me and takes me to a place I never
dreamed I would go

# Acknowledgements

Thank you to all our contributors, for having the courage to share their fantastic work, and to Alice Baxter for the beautiful cover art.

Thank you to all at Converge for all they've done to support this production.

Thank you to the Igen Trust for resourcing and encouraging us.

And finally, thanks to our production team of Helen, William, Nicky, Georgia, Gavin and Rob for being the intrepid crew for this year's bumper voyage of the Great Ship Overly Ambitious!

# About Our Authors

**ANDA BARASKINA** now lives in York, has participated some of the most interesting Converge courses and is looking forward to the next ones.

**ANN N** Studied Creative Writing: Inspirations, through Converge Connected.

**CAROL** is a disabled mum who attends a gym regularly and lives with a lot of pain, but refuses to give up and let life beat her. Her stubborn nature will always shine through.

**CAT EASTERBROOK** is a writer and support worker from York. She started dreaming of writing a book as a child and that dream has recently been rekindled by Converge. Revived and inspired by nature, she can often be found at the Yorkshire coast in her campervan, accompanied by her furry pal, Juno.

**CHAD COPLEY** has been part of Converge for two years now and he writes about relationships with friends and family. He wrote the piece in this anthology because he was trying to understand his thoughts and feelings about his best friend and imagine what she might say in response.

**CHRISTINA** lives in Yorkshire. She likes to ride her dragon Cynthia (evenings mostly) while eating apple pie and drinking strawberry milkshakes, while Cynthia likes to spin covering Christina in the above like a speckled work of art. The inspiration for this piece comes from a word mentioned in class by one of the students. Alongside her writing, Christina likes to paint pictures of birds, flowers, fluffy stuff she's taken when out walking. She also likes to fantasise about winning the lottery, but then who doesn't. Long live the escapism of Creative Writing.

**DAWN SKELTON** resides on the Northern English Coast and is a compassionate writer, poet and artist with a profound love for nature. Creative expression has been a pivotal lifeline, aiding her in both personal discovery and in connecting with a broader cultural community. In solidifying her role as a storyteller of experiences Dawn aspires to inspire others to embrace their voices and stories. Dawn has participated in York St John University Creative writing conference celebrating CWH series. Dawn has deep gratitude of continued educational opportunities offered by Converge. Dawn is currently working on an illustrated poetry book and autobiography. In a new venture in podcasting Dawn aims to show the power of creative therapy in a diverse multidimensional communitive platform.

**ELAINE KELLY** studied at York St John University and is a Converge Tutor. Her favourite quote is 'When writing the story of your life, don't let anyone else hold the pen'.

**ELLIE** lives in York and works for the Discovery Hub at Converge. She loves spending time with dogs and has a keen interest in paper and maritime disasters.

**EMILY POLIS** is a third year occupational therapy student visiting from Pacific University, Oregon. She is originally from Los Angeles, California but has been living in Oregon for the past seven years. Emily has been enjoying her time in York completing her capstone project with Converge and will be so sad to leave at the end of the summer! In her free time, she enjoys making art, spending time in nature, traveling, listening to music, and laughing with friends.

**ESTHER CLARE GRIFFITHS** is a writer and songwriter. She loves to write with her black Labrador snuggled up next to her – he's a great audience and never quick to judge! Her debut novel, *Eliza Quinn Defies Her Destiny* is set in Northern Ireland in the 1920s and is a lyrical, gripping tale of love, loss and friendship. Available via Amazon on Kindle and in paperback (https://amzn.eu/d/2rvjuZ9). Esther has had her songs played regularly on BBC radio and her fourth album is due for release in late 2023. Have a listen to her music atwww.estherclare.bandcamp.com. Esther is currently writing her memoirs of growing up in a tiny cottage in the rolling hills of Northern Ireland - firm friends, close family, the dread of school in Belfast, and long winding walks in search of wine gums! Esther loves her work at Converge as Song writing tutor and a leader of Communitas choir.

**EVE WHEELER** is 24 years old and lives in York, at home with her parents, her brother and a cavalier spaniel poodle crossover doggy named Charlie. Eve was originally born in London, however after having lived in York for 18 years she has fully converted herself as being a proud northerner with a subtle hint of southern flair. As of now, Eve has been a member of Converge for just over 2 years. She currently attends the Creative Writing Inspirations course alongside being a member of the Out of Character performing arts company here at Converge. At home she can often be found listening to podcasts with an occasional session of (variable in quality) sing song merged somewhere in between.

**GEORGIA CONLON** is a poet, tutor, barefoot runner and carnivore. She is the creator of Georgia's Poetry Workshop podcast, and is currently completing her MA in Writing Poetry at Newcastle University.

**GRAHAM WHITTON** studied media in Durham before going on to complete a degree in Counselling and Mental Health at York. He enjoyed his best placement with Converge where he was a volunteer supporting creative writing groups. He enjoys writing short stories in his spare time. Other hobbies include film, hiking and hanging out with friends.

**HAZEL CORNHILL** is a campaigner and podcaster who has written multiple blogs for a variety of charities, about their experience of mental illness. The piece in this book is their first foray into the realms of poetry.

**HELEN KENWRIGHT** is a writer, fangirl, gamer and musician who ran away to York from Croydon many decades ago. It was the best escape she ever made. She writes speculative fiction, romance and is currently working on a novel about secular cults. There's usually dragons.

**HOLLY.** Poet. Watching the world from a window.

Its 1961, a sunny Sunday afternoon in North Yorkshire welcomes the cries of **KEVIN KELD**. Over the coming years he would bounce around the planet leaving a trail of hilarious adventures and jolly japes for the entire world to see. One time owner of the largest motorcycle dismantlers in North Yorkshire and freelance writer for the international motorcycle press, the humble motorcycle is etched firmly into that part of the brain normally reserved for 'amorous activity'. His last book, The Motorcycle Undertaker related many tales of derring do and tomfoolery from his 45 year association with the two wheeled brute. His follow up book is well under way and more hilarious tales are being consigned to paper as we speak. His passions are many and varied. From Gothic architecture through to disused railways, from progressive rock music to Steampunk and all points between. An unnatural obsession with the Cadbury's Caramel bunny had also been rumoured but as yet no one has been able to obtain proof. Kevin lives with a Tsum Tsum called Mr Thing and an Alsatian named Arthur Morgan.

**JACOB HUITT** is someone who grew up in Lethbridge, Alberta, Canada, only to find himself back in his birthplace of York, England. After spending his childhood in the beautiful Canadian landscapes, he took the brave step of returning to York to pursue a better education. Along the way, he faced daunting challenges like social anxiety, C-PTSD, loneliness, and the bewildering effects of culture shock. But Jacob didn't let these hurdles hold him back. With sheer determination, he embarked on a journey of self-improvement, overcoming each obstacle one by one and embracing personal growth with unwavering resilience.

To his possible credit, **jim mcnalley** has but a reasonable conceit of himself.

**JAMES WILSON** has enjoyed two years of creative writing with Converge. In his spare time, he plays guitar, reads and likes games consoles. He lives twelve miles from York. He often visits the Yorkshire coast and sometimes writes about that. He has studied the course by post and hopes to continue with Converge.

**JOHN F. GOODFELLOW** is a South African born emerging screenwriter & poet. He lives in York and suffers from Bipolar Affective Disorder. He is also an artist, painting large acrylic abstract work. A true Renaissance Man.

**JUNIOR MARK CRYLE**, The Man, The Myth, The Dragon Fanatic. His voice has become distinct within Converge, his accent is unknown. Junior has been published in CWH since Volume 2, growing with experience in hopes of entertaining readers through laughter and adventure. (But mainly laughter, Junior clarifies.) Junior presented a workshop, *Dragons in Fiction* for the YSJ Converge Creative Writing Conference in 2023.

**KAI-LATIFA** moved to York as a teenager. She enjoys reading and playing video games in her spare time. She hopes to one day publish a book filled with her ramblings.

**KAREN WILSON** lives in York and works for the Discovery Hub at Converge. She welcomes the opportunity to take part in Converge courses as part of her job role, and especially enjoys Creative Writing.

**KATE HIGNETT** was inspired by Helen's course on Feminism. She lives in York and has two black cats, Wilbur and Kitweazle.

**KEITH MYERS** lives in York. He likes doing poetry. A mature student, he has studied Creative Writing for a number of years.

**LYNNE PARKIN** has been a part of this universe for six decades and shares her home with her husband and Bedlington Terrier Ludo Her children and grandchildren are a big part of her life. She loves children's literature and a good murder mystery. Binge watching TV crime drama series is her guilty pleasure as are profiteroles. It's all about the simple things in life.

**MEG PADGETT** is a performance artist, based in York. Throughout her degree at York St. John studying Drama:

Education and Community, she has been a student volunteer with Converge, supporting varying courses, including theatre and creative writing. She has loved being a part of the creative writing course, as creativity is her outlet, and she finds great catharsis through putting things down onto a page, no matter the format! The piece she has written for this anthology is very special to her, as she wrote it in dedication to her Great Aunt, Sybil.

**MICHAEL FAIRCLOUGH** currently has nothing to aim for having released his first book *Making Ends Meat* in April of 2023 (https://tinyurl.com/4pvn8zkn). Not even one of them troughs you find in pub toilets. Michael also regularly experiences self-loafing. That's the act of dressing up like a loaf of bread and shouting at people in supermarkets to cut you. You can find more of Michael's writing in the previous Creative Writing Heals books except for Vol 1. Some people accuse Michael of being dropped on his head as a child but it was actually a lot more recently.

**MILLY** lives in Yorkshire. One day she might find herself committing to a singular writing project, yet it evades her still as of now. To help with relaxation, she now indulges in herbal tea and consumes so-bad-it's-good media by the dozen. As a child, her dream was to become a fairy princess, and as that hasn't panned out, she's figured writing about them is the perfect form of therapy. She also holds the coveted title of being her parents Favourite Daughter. Her only sibling is a younger brother.

**NAOMI NUNNS** studied Music, Art and Introduction to Feminism courses at Converge. She is now taking her studies further and currently undertaking an Undergraduate Certificate of Higher Education in the Study of Early Medieval and Medieval England with the Institute of Continuing Education, University of Cambridge, and hopes to continue studying within her interests of History, the Arts and Literature.

**NICKY KIPPAX** is a poet from Yorkshire. Her poetry can be found in many anthologies and magazines including, most recently, Poetry News, The Rialto and The Alchemy

Spoon. Her work has been shortlisted for the Bridport Prize, the Bath Fiction Prize and she is a 2022 Northern Writer Award winner. Nicky runs a family bakery and is currently editing her first collection.

**OLYA**, having fulfilled her teenage dream of ending the Cold War, has moved on to creating florid paintings and torrid prose. She's even ventured into the treacherous waters of poetic expression.

**PAUL FRANCIS WORT** was born in 1973. His childhood saw him living in a council house on the outskirts of Swanage, a small village in North Wales, a children's home in Dorchester and a foster home in Bournemouth. He studied at Winchester and has a First-Class degree in English with American Studies. He has worked in administration for the HE Sector and the NHS. He has also sold ice creams. His hobbies include making primitive home music recordings and, for several years, he was keyboardist in the Converge band 1/2/6. He has lived in York for the past 25 years.

**SAMANTHA** lives in York with her dog Douglas and three cats. She enjoys cycling, painting and being in nature, off the beaten track. Since joining Converge she has also discovered the joy of creative writing. She loves spending time with dogs and has a keen interest in paper and maritime disasters.

**TAMAR** has a lovely little family and a puppy called Blue. Life is like a rollercoaster, and using a pen (that she likes to call her wand) helps her to express herself. She hopes you enjoy her work.

**VIRGINIA SELLAR-EDMUNDS** still lives in York with her wife, and still believes that 'Yorkshireness' is handed down from mother to daughter. Virginia has had two previous Miss Nicely stories published in *Creative Writing Heals 5* and had some poems published in *Root Maps*, in 1998. Virginia is a passionate cook, and particularly likes to cook authentic Indian food. She is proud to recount how during an 8-week period of living alone while her wife was in hospital, she cooked Indian every day, and never repeated a recipe. Virginia has three adult children, who may well find themselves in a future Miss Nicely story.

**WILLIAM DAVIDSON** lives in York and is a Converge tutor. He studied Creative Writing at York St John and won the inaugural Bath Flash Fiction Award. His stories have been published in various anthologies including Creative Writing Heals.

# About Converge

Converge is a partnership between York St John University and mental health service providers in the York region. It offers high quality educational opportunities to those who use NHS and non-statutory mental health services and who are 18 years and over.

Converge was established in 2008 from a simple idea: to offer good quality courses in a university setting to local people who use mental health services taught by students and staff. The development of Converge has progressively demonstrated the potential of offering educational opportunities to people who use mental health services, delivered by students and staff and held on a university campus. This has become the key principle which, today, remains at the heart of Converge. Born of a unique collaboration between the NHS and York St John University, Converge continues to deliver educational opportunities for people with mental health problems.

We offer work-based experience to university students involved in the programme. All classes are taught by undergraduate and postgraduate students, staff and, increasingly people who have lived experience of mental ill health. We have developed a solid track record of delivering quality courses. Careful support and mentoring underpin our work, thereby allowing students to experiment with their own ideas and creativity whilst gaining real world experience in the community. This undoubtedly enhances their employability in an increasingly competitive market.

As a leader in the field, Converge develops symbiotic projects and partnerships which are driven by innovation and best practice. The result is twofold: a rich and exciting educational opportunity for people with mental health problems alongside authentic and practical work experience for university students.

The aims of Converge are to:

- Work together as artists and students
- Build a community where we learn from each other
- Engage and enhance the university and wider community
- Provide a supportive and inclusive environment
- Respect others and value ourselves
- Above all, strive to be ordinary, extraordinary yet ourselves

# About the Writing Tree

The Writing Tree is dedicated to the support and nurturing of creative writers. Founded in 2011, the Writing Tree offers tuition, e-format conversion and editing services and publishes work by community groups and other new writers.

The guiding principles of the Writing Tree are that creative writing has importance independent of subject, purpose or audience, and that everyone has the right to write, and to write what they wish.

The Writing Tree is honoured to publish 'Creative Writing Heals' for Converge. All profits from the book are donated to further the efforts of Converge writers.

You can find out more about the Writing Tree at www.writingtree.co.uk.

Printed in Great Britain
by Amazon